STALLION IN THE STORM

Suddenly, the quiet atmosphere exploded in noisy confusion. A clatter of hooves rang through the air outside the barn while, inside, the horses began to neigh and squeal. They wheeled around, all of them now kicking out against the sides of their stalls.

'What's happening?' cried James in alarm.

'Come on, let's go and see!' Mandy replied, rushing out towards the yard with James close on her heels. She blinked her eyes in the sudden glare of daylight – then froze in horror.

A riderless horse was heading straight for her, galloping blindly towards the entrance of the barn. It was fully saddled and bridled, stirrup irons flapping wildly against sweaty, foaming flanks. Panic showed in its rolling eyes and snorting nostrils, and the thundering clatter of its pounding hooves filled the whole yard.

'Mandy, look out!' she heard her father cry from behind her . . .

Animal Ark series

LUCY DANIELS

Stallion
– in the –
Storm

Illustrations by Ann Baum

Hodder
Children's
Books

a division of Hodder Headline Limited

Special thanks to Jenny Walters
Thanks also to C. J. Hall, B.Vet.Med., M.R.C.V.S., for reviewing
the veterinary information contained in this book.

Animal Ark is a trademark of Working Partners Ltd
Text copyright © 1999 Working Partners Ltd
Created by Working Partners Ltd, London W6 0QT
Original series created by Ben M. Baglio
Illustrations copyright © 1999 Ann Baum

First published in Great Britain in 1999
by Hodder Children's Books

The right of Lucy Daniels to be identified as the author of this work
has been asserted by her in accordance with the Copyright,
Designs and Patents Act 1988.

15 14 13 12 11 10 9 8 7 6

A Catalogue record for this book is available from the British Library

ISBN 0 340 73602 X

Typeset by Avon DataSet Ltd, Bidford-on-Avon, Warks

Printed and bound in Great Britain by
Clays Ltd, St Ives plc

The paper and board used in this paperback by
Hodder Children's Books are natural recyclable products
made from wood grown in sustainable forests. The manufacturing
processes conform to the environmental regulations
of the country of origin.

Hodder Children's Books
a division of Hodder Headline Limited
338 Euston Road
London NW1 3BH

One

'Mandy, can you spare a minute?' Jean Knox, the receptionist at Animal Ark, put her head round the kitchen door. She had a pen behind her ear and a frazzled expression on her face. 'Everything's suddenly gone haywire.'

'Sure.' Mandy Hope closed the book she'd been leafing through and jumped up from her chair at the big pine kitchen table. She followed Jean through into the bright, modern vet's practice that was housed behind the old cottage where the Hope family lived. Mandy's father, Adam Hope, was taking Saturday morning surgery and it seemed to have been going on for ever.

'Do you know which formula of dog food is for older puppies?' Jean asked over her shoulder. 'The instructions on the bags aren't very clear. And I can't find Mr Pickard's records anywhere!' she added worriedly.

'Oh, the yellow bags of food are for older puppies and young dogs,' Mandy replied. 'I remember Mum telling someone else.'

At the counter, a bouncy young golden retriever was frisking around his distracted owner's legs, winding his lead into knots.

Mandy walked over to the sacks of dried dog food sold at the surgery and took one of the yellow bags over to Jean. 'Just right for you,' she said, giving the playful dog a pat.

'Thanks, love, that's one problem solved,' said Jean, ringing up the price on the till. 'Now if we can just sort Mr Pickard out . . .'

Walter Pickard was sitting on a chair with his old cat, Tom, glaring balefully out of a wire travelling cage on his lap.

'Hi, Mr Pickard,' Mandy called. She walked over to have a look at Tom, who sat twitching his tail and looking grumpy. As she got closer, Mandy noticed he had a torn ear. 'Oh, Tom! Have you been fighting again?' she scolded gently. 'You're going to get into real trouble one day.'

The big black-and-white moggy just stared at her and blinked. Walter Pickard smiled and shook his head. 'He never learns, silly old thing.'

Mandy nodded. She hated seeing animals in pain, but she knew her father would soon have Tom patched up and made comfortable.

She found Mr Pickard's records under 'W' instead of 'P' in the jam-packed filing cabinet and laid them on the desk, just in time for Simon the practice nurse to snatch them up as he came into the reception area.

'Thanks, Mandy, you're a star,' he told her as he ushered Mr Pickard and Tom back through into the treatment room.

'Remind Dad we're meant to be going soon!' Mandy called after him. But she knew her father would take just as long as he needed to. After all, sick animals and worried owners couldn't be hurried. She would just have to be patient.

Mandy was sorting out some other files that

had been put back in the wrong places when she caught sight of her best friend, James Hunter, hastily parking his bike against the wall outside. He waved at her through the window.

'You go off now, Mandy,' Jean told her. 'I think the rush is over. And thanks – I don't know what I'd have done without you!'

'Am I late?' James asked anxiously as he came into the surgery. 'I was worried you'd be waiting for me.'

Mandy shook her head. 'Dad's still seeing patients,' she told him. 'I don't think he'll be much longer, though. There's only a couple of hamsters and a cat to go. Do you want to go through to the kitchen? I got this great book about the Grand National out of the library – come and have a look!'

Ever since Mr Hope had told Mandy that he had been asked to fill in as the vet at Folan's racing stables, all she could think about was horses. Mandy loved all the animals who came through the doors of Animal Ark, but a purebred racehorse was something special. She couldn't wait to get close to one, and now was her chance. They were actually going to the stables – just as soon as her father was ready . . .

'All right, you two,' announced Adam Hope as he came into the large oak-beamed kitchen. 'Surgery's finished, so we can be off to Folan's. If you still want to go, that is?' He raised one dark eyebrow as he looked at Mandy and James.

'Oh, Dad, what do you think?' Mandy exclaimed.

'Well . . . maybe it might be better if I went on my own later in the week,' said Mr Hope, with a twinkle in his eye.

'Ha ha, very funny,' said Mandy. 'We've been looking forward to this for ages, Dad! You can't put us off now.'

'We've found out a lot about thoroughbreds, Mr Hope,' said James, looking alarmed at the thought of missing the trip. 'Dad and I found a racing website on the Internet last night. We'll be careful not to get in the way.'

'He's only joking, James,' said Mandy, swinging open the heavy kitchen door and stepping out into crisp early autumn sunshine. 'He promised we could go with him, as it's the weekend. And Mum doesn't want us getting under her feet today.'

Emily Hope had disappeared into the study early that morning clutching a pile of papers. 'If I don't catch up on this paperwork, Animal Ark's going to come to a grinding halt,' she told her husband sternly. 'And you treating animals for free half the time doesn't help.'

Mandy and her father had exchanged guilty grins as the study door closed behind Mrs Hope with a businesslike thud. They knew she never asked for payment from the animal sanctuary either.

Mr Hope looked at his watch. 'Can you and James have a quick look at Rolo for me while I get my things ready, Mandy love?' he said. 'There's some new laser equipment I might just sling in the back of the Land-rover. Shouldn't think I'll need to use it, but you never know.'

'What's the matter with Rolo?' asked James as he and Mandy walked over to the open-air compound to look at the roly-poly little Shetland pony.

'Laminitis – inflammation of the feet,' Mandy replied. 'He's been fed too much and hasn't had his hooves picked out for ages, poor thing. Still, he's looking a lot better than he did yesterday. Let's give him a quick brush while we're waiting. That might make him feel a bit happier.'

Nothing made Mandy angrier than seeing animals suffer because they hadn't been looked after properly, and she muttered crossly to herself as she groomed Rolo's rough coat. The pony was still leaning back a little as he stood, trying to take the weight off the sensitive parts of his feet, but at least his hooves weren't as warm as they had been the day before, which meant that the inflammation was going down.

'Those painkillers seem to be doing the trick,' said Mr Hope, joining them. 'I've had a word with his owners about changing his diet and looking after his feet a bit better. He should be fine in a few days.'

'Well then, what are we waiting for?' said Mandy, giving Rolo a finishing stroke, then linking her arm through her father's. 'Let's go and see these racehorses!'

After a couple of tries, the Land-rover roared

into life and swung out into the lane, past the carved wooden Animal Ark sign, which swung gently in the freshening autumn breeze. Summer was definitely over.

'Must take this old thing for a service,' muttered Mr Hope absent-mindedly, scratching his dark beard, as they passed through the village of Welford and headed out towards the rolling Yorkshire countryside.

'Tell us a bit more about the stables, Dad,' Mandy asked, checking yet again to make sure she hadn't forgotten her camera. There were just a few exposures left on the roll of film and she was hoping to get some great shots.

'Well, I don't know that much about the place myself,' Mr Hope replied. 'Old Mr Folan died last year and his son took over. Things seem to have gone a bit quiet since then, but Folan's has always had a good name in the business. It's a small stable, but they've kept and trained some wonderful winners, for the top owners.'

'What, like the Aga Khan and Sheikh Mohammed?' James asked eagerly.

'Not quite,' Mr Hope laughed. 'But we should see some fine horses all the same.'

Mandy caught James's eye and gave him a broad grin. He loved animals nearly as much as she did.

'There won't be any chance of riding though,' Mr Hope warned. 'Thoroughbreds can be very highly strung and they're strong too.'

'No, Dad, don't worry, we weren't expecting to,' Mandy replied. Both she and James had learned to ride at Bennett's stables. They had become quite skilful, but they knew enough not to even think of asking if they might take a racehorse for a gallop. 'I just want to see them in action,' she went on. 'And maybe we can help with grooming or feeding while you have a look around. Is there anything in particular they need you for?'

'I don't think so,' her father replied. 'I'm really just holding the fort for them until they can find a specialist horse vet. They'll probably just want me for emergencies, not day-to-day care. Accidents, colic, leg problems, sprained tendons – that kind of thing. I'm looking forward to seeing how the yard's run, though. Should be fascinating!'

They each lapsed into their own thoughts as

Mr Hope steered the Land-rover along the narrow country lanes.

Half an hour later, they passed a good-sized field on the right, with a dark mass of wood behind and a sturdy wooden fence running along the boundary, separating it from the road. The field seemed to be empty – but then Mandy caught a flash of white out of the corner of her eye.

Turning her head, she saw the figure of a horse, standing stock-still. It was a large stallion, with a dazzling silver-white coat. Perfectly balanced, it was standing with one hind leg bent at the knee, the tip of its hoof resting lightly on the ground. And it was looking straight at Mandy. There was something so direct and intent in its gaze. Mandy stared back, transfixed, her heart thumping in her chest.

As luck would have it, the Land-rover slowed down just then to turn into a long driveway, signposted to Folan's stables. Mandy was able to raise her camera quickly, frame the beautiful animal in the centre of the viewfinder and take a picture.

The spell broken, she turned to James and

gave him a nudge. 'Look, James!' she said. 'Isn't that a fantastic-looking horse?'

Pushing his glasses back into place, James looked up from the copy of *Horse and Hound* he'd brought with him and gazed around. 'Where?' he said.

Mandy looked – but now all she could see as the Land-rover sped up the drive was acres of green grass. Not a horse in sight.

'It's disappeared!' she said, craning around to look behind. 'But it was here just a second ago – a big grey stallion. I took a photo of him.'

'Well, I'll see him later then,' James answered calmly. 'He's probably just gone behind a tree or something. I'm sure we'll meet plenty more. Look, here we are!'

The Land-rover swung into Folan's stables. Mr Hope turned off the engine and the three of them sat for a little while, looking around.

Mandy was the first to break the silence. 'It's not quite what I was expecting,' she said doubtfully. She'd imagined a bustling place, with stablehands busy grooming and mucking out, while jockeys trotted by on elegant long-legged thoroughbreds. Folan's yard was not like that at all. It was so quiet and empty! 'Where *is* everyone?' she asked.

James shrugged. He could usually come up with an answer for everything, but now even he seemed lost for words.

Deep puddles pitted the ground, where rainwater was spilling noisily from a blocked gutter. Mandy noticed a messy muck heap sprawled against a tumbledown brick wall, and an unhooked door banging eerily in the wind. It was all very strange. Strange, and forbidding.

'It does look a bit grim,' Mr Hope agreed. 'Come on, though, let's explore.'

The three of them jumped down from the Land-rover.

'That must be where they stable the horses,' Mr Hope said, pointing to a large barn at the top end of the yard. Inside, two rows of about ten stalls faced each other, either side of a wide central aisle. They might have been empty, yet Mandy could hear the stamping of hooves and, now and then, a whinny from deep inside.

'Why aren't the horses looking out to see what's going on?' she asked, worriedly. 'It's like they're in hiding. You'd think there'd be one or two who'd want to say hello.'

Mr Hope scratched his beard thoughtfully. 'Let's see if we can take a quick tour of the barn on our own,' he said. 'Might be interesting to see how the horses react to strangers.'

They walked over to the barn, James and Mandy sticking close to Mr Hope's side.

'I brought an apple with me,' Mandy told him. 'It won't stretch very far, but it might come in handy to start off with.'

'Well, every little helps,' said Mr Hope. 'Something tells me these horses aren't feeling very friendly today. They may need some persuading to come and say hello.'

'Shouldn't we ask before we give them anything to eat?' asked James.

'Well, strictly speaking, we should,' Mr Hope replied, 'but I don't think an apple will do too much harm. And I would like to see one or two of the horses without the stable manager looking over my shoulder.'

As they entered the barn, Mandy took in a deep lungful of the rich straw, sweat and leather smell that is always in the air wherever horses are kept. Then she wrinkled her nose. 'I think they might need some help mucking out,' she whispered to James. 'It smells like it hasn't been done for a while.'

'Yes, I know what you mean,' he replied, just as quietly. 'There's a wheelbarrow over there, but no one seems to be working today.'

Mr Hope went up to the first stall. 'Come on, boy,' he called to the chestnut horse inside it who was eyeing him warily from the shadows. 'We're not going to hurt you.'

'Look, Dad, he's called Jupiter,' said Mandy. 'His name's on the door of the stall. Come here, Jupiter, and say hello.'

But Jupiter wasn't going anywhere in a hurry.

'I think we may need your apple, Mandy,' Mr Hope said to her. 'Do you want to have a try?'

Mandy nodded and took the apple out of her pocket. 'Jupiter, look what I've got for you,' she wheedled, biting off a chunk and holding it flat on her outstretched palm.

Ears lying back along his neck, Jupiter inched his way towards Mandy as she carried on talking softly. He looked ready to spring back at any moment, but her calm, quiet tone gradually seemed to be winning him over. He blew down

his nose, tickling Mandy's hand, then twitched his soft, whiskery lips and daintily took the piece of apple. As he crunched, his ears flicked forward in a more friendly way, but he still eyed them warily.

'That's better,' said Mr Hope, rubbing the horse's satiny neck. 'I didn't like the look of those ears, laid right back like that. But he's a nice old fellow. Aren't you, Jupiter?' He carried on chatting calmly to the horse, looking him over as far as he could.

'*Is* he old?' said James, risking a quick stroke himself.

'No, he's a youngster,' Mr Hope replied. 'I'd say he's probably no more than about two or three. Let's have a look at his mouth. Yes, see – he's got a couple of milk teeth still. The others are pretty straight, and not worn down at all.'

'He's beautiful, isn't he?' said James, looking at the horse's dark, intelligent eyes and glossy brown coat. 'He certainly is nervous, though. I wonder why?'

'I don't know,' Mr Hope replied. 'But I want to find out.' He turned away and began to walk down the wide central aisle of the barn, towards a dull thudding noise that had started up near the back, echoing over and over again.

'What on earth's that?' Mandy called to her father.

'One of the horses is kicking its stable door,' he replied. 'They develop these habits if they're bored, shut up too long in the same place.'

Mandy sighed and looked deep into Jupiter's dark eyes. 'What's the matter here, boy?' she asked him. 'What's making you all miserable?' But Jupiter just blew down his nose at her and turned his head away, retreating to the back of the stall again.

And then, suddenly, the quiet atmosphere exploded in noisy confusion. A clatter of hooves rang through the air outside the barn while, inside, the horses began to neigh and squeal. They wheeled around, all of them now kicking out against the sides of their stalls.

'What's happening?' cried James in alarm.

'Come on, let's go and see!' Mandy replied, rushing out towards the yard with James close on her heels. She blinked her eyes in the sudden glare of daylight – then froze in horror.

A riderless horse was heading straight for her, galloping blindly towards the entrance of the barn. It was fully saddled and bridled, stirrup irons flapping wildly against sweaty, foaming flanks. Panic showed in its rolling eyes and snorting nostrils, and the thundering clatter of its pounding hooves filled the whole yard.

'Mandy, look out!' she heard her father cry from behind her.

'Get back, Mandy!' James shouted.

But there was no time to run. Mandy crouched down against the barn wall, her arms over her head to try and protect herself. Time seemed to stand still as she waited for the impact she felt certain would follow . . .

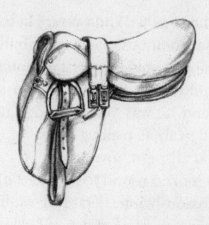

Two

Mandy hugged her arms tighter over her head as she braced herself for the moment when those galloping hooves would smash into her body.

But it didn't come. To her amazement, she heard the horse suddenly skid to a halt, its metal shoes clattering on the stony ground.

Looking up, Mandy saw it snort and rear up in front of the entrance to the barn, then wheel round and dash back down to the yard. It ended up in one corner like a hunted beast, shivering and rolling its eyes.

'Easy there, boy. Whoa now, Hadrian.' Two men had rushed out of a nearby building and were circling around the terrified animal, trying to take hold of it. Seconds later a stable lad arrived, and he was able to dodge nearer the horse and grab its trailing reins.

'Are you all right, love?'

Mandy looked round to see her father's face staring anxiously into hers. Her wildly beating heart began to slow down. She let out her breath, grateful for his arm round her shoulders as he helped her to get up. 'Phew! I thought I was done for!' she said, stumbling a little over the words.

'You're not the only one,' Mr Hope replied hoarsely.

Mandy noticed that he'd gone very pale, as had James, who was hovering worriedly at her side.

'Sure you're OK?' James asked her. 'I was certain the horse was going to crash straight into you!'

'Me too!' Mandy said shakily. 'Why do you think he bolted like that? He looked terrified! And what's happened to his rider?'

'We'll let someone else worry about that,' said her father. 'Right now, I'm more concerned about you.'

'Oh, I'm fine, Dad,' Mandy insisted, brushing some dirt off the knees of her jeans. Her legs were still trembling, but she was beginning to breathe more normally. 'Really, I mean it.'

She looked back down to the yard to see what was happening. The stable lad was still trying to calm the frantic horse, while one of the men who'd rushed out was climbing into a red van parked in the yard.

His companion, an older man, was walking quickly up towards them, looking worried. 'Harry Johnson, stable manager,' he said, holding out his hand to Mr Hope. 'Sorry about that little drama! We had no idea anyone was here – is everyone OK?'

Mr Hope stepped forward. 'Adam Hope, the relief vet,' he said, shaking hands with Mr Johnson. 'And this is my daughter Mandy, and her friend James. You were expecting us, I think.' The stable manager nodded to each of them as Mr Hope continued seriously, 'No harm done, but your runaway certainly gave us a scare. There could have been a nasty accident – a very jumpy horse you've got there.'

Mr Johnson ran a hand uneasily through his thinning grey hair. 'He's not jumpy as a rule,' he said. 'But he's so hard to handle these days . . .' He turned to Mandy. 'I'm sure Hadrian wouldn't have hurt you on purpose,' he said apologetically. 'But it must have been quite a shock for you.'

Mandy nodded and smiled. 'I'm OK, though,' she replied.

'Maybe it's all these wretched storms we've been having,' Mr Johnson suggested. 'None of the horses seems to be able to settle afterwards.'

'Storms?' asked Mr Hope, surprised. 'I don't think we've had any in Welford, and it's not so very far away.'

'Oh, we tend to get them at night,' explained Mr Johnson. 'You're probably fast asleep in bed. Best place to be, if you ask me.' He laughed – a little nervously, Mandy thought. 'It gives me the creeps up here sometimes, I can tell you, with the wind howling round and the stall doors banging the way they do.'

A sudden thought occurred to Mandy. 'Who

was riding Hadrian?' she asked. 'Do you think he's OK?'

'Oh, I should say so,' Mr Johnson replied. 'Pete Marshall was riding him – and he's had quite a few falls in his time. Jim, our other jockey, has taken the van out to find him. He got thrown in the woods too, last week, so he'll know where to look.' The stable manager scratched his head. 'Something about the woods seems to be spooking Hadrian lately. Heaven knows what.'

The stable boy led the sweating horse past them, towards the barn. Hadrian looked exhausted. His eyes were dull and listless, and his ears twitched nervously.

Mr Johnson reached out and gave Hadrian an affectionate stroke. 'Daft animal, aren't you, lad?' he said. 'Sponge him down after you've unsaddled him, Tom. Then he can go back in the stall with a sweat sheet on to calm down for a while.'

Tom nodded, rubbing the horse's nose affectionately.

'Tom's my best stable lad,' Mr Johnson said, turning to Mr Hope. 'He's one of the few who've stayed with us since . . .' The stable manager seemed to think better of saying any more. 'Now, how about a cup of tea down in the office?' he said briskly, changing the subject.

'If it's all right with you, Mr Johnson,' Adam Hope said firmly, 'I think I'd like to take a proper look around now. Do you want to do the honours? We could start with the horses in the barn, and I can check Hadrian over when he's ready.'

'Of course,' said Mr Johnson, rubbing his hands together nervously. 'That's what you're here for, after all.'

'Can we come too, Dad?' Mandy asked.

'Well, if you're sure you're up to it,' her father replied. He looked questioningly at her. 'Or you could find a quiet place to sit and get your breath back.'

'I'm fine, and I'd sooner come along,' Mandy told him. She could tell from her father's voice that he had more than a few misgivings about what they'd seen of the stables so far. And she wanted to find out more about what was going on, too.

'Right then, let's get started,' Harry Johnson

said, leading them all back towards the barn.

Mandy felt something nudge at her ankle and, still on edge after her ordeal, gave a little scream. She whirled round to see a brown-and-white terrier trotting along behind them.

'Don't worry, that's only Queenie,' Harry Johnson said, smiling. 'She helps me to run the place. She won't hurt you!'

'No, I'm sure she won't!' Mandy said, laughing at her mistake. She bent down and held out her hand. The dog licked her fingers, its stumpy tail wagging, then trotted along with them into the barn.

'Now for a proper look round,' Mandy murmured to James. Slowly, they made their way down the aisle with Queenie at their heels, some distance behind her father and Mr Johnson. The two men were deep in conversation. 'Perhaps Dad can get to the bottom of all this,' she added, watching them.

'I still don't understand about this storm business,' James replied with a frown. 'Surely we'd have heard the wind, even if it was in the middle of the night?'

But Mandy was too busy looking at the horses

to worry about the weather. She gazed at the rows of stalls, and the elegant, leggy thoroughbreds who stood warily inside them. Their glossy coats ranged through every shade of light and dark, from the palest sandy dun to the deepest black. Taking out her camera, she took a couple of photographs, though the light was so dim inside the stables she didn't know how they'd turn out.

'Don't all these names sound wonderful?' she said to James. 'Listen – Midnight Runner, Fair Lady, Double-Decker, Shooting Star . . . I wonder how many races they've won between them?'

She stopped at one of the stalls and gazed at a fine-looking bright bay horse. He fidgeted from one leg to the other, swishing his tail, and stared back at her with soft brown eyes.

'Oh, he's lovely, isn't he?' James breathed, coming to stand next to her. 'Pilgrim's Progress, it says on the door. He looks so intelligent – like he knows just what's going on.'

'I wish he could talk,' Mandy said. 'There are a lot of questions I'd like to ask him.'

'About why the horses seem so jumpy, you mean?' James said.

Mandy nodded, clicking her fingers to see if Pilgrim would come any closer. 'Maybe this barn has got something to do with it. Don't you think it feels a bit – *spooky*, somehow?' She looked down the echoing, gloomy central corridor and shivered. 'Perhaps the horses feel it too.'

James looked a bit sceptical. 'Come on, Mandy,' he said. 'It does feel a bit cold and miserable in here, but aren't you jumping to conclusions?'

Mandy was about to reply when Mr Hope called over, 'Come over here, you two!'

Harry Johnson was opening one of the stall doors and leading out the horse inside.

'Oh, it's Hadrian!' Mandy said. 'Come on, James – let's see how he is!'

'Be careful,' James said, catching her arm. 'You don't know what he's going to do!'

'Don't worry about this fellow, he's quiet as a lamb now,' Mr Hope called back, as James and Mandy came over. 'I thought you might like a closer look at a thoroughbred.'

Mandy did feel a little wary at first, but she soon saw that her father was right. Hadrian stood there in a sweat sheet stuffed with a layer of straw, to ensure he didn't catch cold, his head hanging low. All the fight had gone out of him.

'He doesn't look very happy, does he?' she said sympathetically, rubbing the horse's nose gently. 'Is he ill, do you think?'

'Well, that's what we'll have to find out,' Mr Hope said, taking Hadrian's pulse. He checked his temperature too, then stood a little way behind the horse, watching intently.

'What are you looking for?' James asked.

'I'm watching his breathing,' Mr Hope replied. 'Horses breathe much more slowly than we do, but you should be able to see his ribs rising and falling. Take a look at those legs, too – see how straight his hocks are. They'll support his weight evenly and help him to run fast when he needs to. No, he's certainly a well-made animal. Good conformation is the fancy way of putting it.'

'One of our finest,' said Harry Johnson proudly. 'When he's on form, that is.'

Mandy watched attentively as her father slowly ran his hands down the horse's legs and carefully picked up each one in turn, checking Hadrian's hooves. The horse started back a little at first, but Mr Johnson held him firmly by the leading rein attached to his headcollar and soothed him down.

'Well, I can't find anything much wrong with him,' Mr Hope said eventually, putting down the last leg. 'I'll take a blood sample, though – and from all the other horses, too. Might be a virus of some kind that's hard to pinpoint.'

Harry Johnson groaned. 'Let's hope not!' he

said. 'On top of everything else, that would finish us off.'

Mandy looked at James, raising her eyebrows. What did the stable manager mean by that?

'On top of everything else?' said her father, shooting Harry Johnson a piercing look. 'Is there something else I ought to know?'

There was a short silence, and Mr Johnson shifted awkwardly as three pairs of eyes turned intently towards him. Mandy and James were just as keen as Mr Hope to hear what he had to say.

'Folan's has been having a run of bad luck lately,' the stable manager began carefully, running Hadrian's leading rein back and forth through his hands. 'Something seems to have got into all the horses . . . They're all jumpy, like Hadrian – but they never used to be that way. We've lost a lot of staff because of it. No one wants to work with such nervous horses – and it's showing in the racing results, too. We haven't won a race since . . .' Again, Mr Johnson seemed to pull himself up short, reluctant to say more. 'It's as though the horses have lost heart,' he finished quietly. 'That's the only way I can put it.'

'Well, let's hope your luck will change soon,' Mr Hope said, when it was clear that Harry Johnson had said all he was going to on the matter. 'Now, shall we go and see that lame mare you told me about?'

'Good idea,' said Mr Johnson briskly. 'She's in one of the loose boxes. I'll just put this fellow back and then we can go on down to the yard.'

'You carry on, Dad,' Mandy broke in. 'Perhaps James and I can give Tom a hand with some of the chores – if that's OK with you, Mr Johnson.' She'd just spotted the stable lad on his way back up from the yard.

'Fine,' the stable manager replied, sounding preoccupied. 'You two have a look round – I'm sure Tom can find you plenty to do if you get bored.'

'We'll catch up with you later,' called Mr Hope with a wave. Together, he and Harry Johnson walked out of the far end of the barn, their dark silhouettes framed for a few seconds against the bright daylight outside. Queenie watched them go, then trotted back to stay with James and Mandy. She seemed to have decided she was going to keep an eye on them.

'Do you think there's something Mr Johnson's not telling us?' Mandy asked James when the two men were out of earshot.

'Definitely,' he replied. 'He broke off his explanation twice, did you notice? I'm sure there's something he'd rather we didn't know.'

'I saw Tom coming this way just now,' Mandy went on. 'Perhaps if we help him with his work we might be able to get him talking and find out some more.'

'I'd sooner be outside in the sunshine,' James grumbled, rubbing his arms. 'It's freezing in here!'

'I know,' Mandy said. 'And it's so quiet, too!' Now that her father and Mr Johnson had gone, the barn full of horses had fallen back into an unnatural silence, not a whinny or snort from any of them. It was as though they were watching and waiting. But for what?

Mandy shivered again as she made her way back into the depths of the barn. She stopped and looked curiously at one of the stalls, a large empty one, next to Hadrian's. 'I wonder who this stall belongs to?' she called back to James, gazing over the top of the door and into the dark interior. 'There's no nameplate.'

James and Queenie came over to join her. 'No, but there was once,' he said, pointing to a rectangle of lighter wood high up on the door. 'It's been taken off. I wonder why?'

'Well, it's obviously not being used at the moment,' Mandy said. 'There's not a trace of hay or straw anywhere.'

'Hey, Mandy! Look at those marks!' James suddenly exclaimed, pointing further down the door.

Mandy looked where he was pointing and saw that a series of horseshoe-shaped scars had been gouged out of the wood. 'How weird!' she said. 'It looks as though a horse has been trying to force its way *into* the stall. But why?'

James shook his head, looking puzzled too. 'You'd think the dents would be on the other side of the door – that he'd be trying to kick his way *out* rather than *in*, wouldn't you?'

Mandy bent down for a closer look, tracing the outline of the hoof marks. 'They're enormous,' she said, 'and so deep! Must have been a huge creature.'

She straightened up and stared again over

the top of the door and into the dark stall. But its walls were bare and empty of any clues. At her feet, Queenie growled warily, the hackles along the back of her neck stiff and raised.

'I'm just going to take a quick look inside,' Mandy decided. 'Maybe there's something in there that we can't see from here.' She reached out her hand to the bolt of the door. At once, Queenie burst out into a volley of frantic barking.

'Shh, Queenie!' James said. 'Oh, leave it, Mandy. Queenie is getting into a real state for some reason.'

Stubbornly, Mandy shook her head. 'Just hold her for a minute and I'll slip inside. I won't be long.' She drew back the icy-cold bolt. Then, as she was about to pull open the door, a voice from behind stopped her dead in her tracks.

'What do you think you're doing?' it shouted. 'You can't go in there!'

Three

Mandy whirled around guiltily to find the stable lad, Tom, glaring at her. He set down his wheelbarrow and, striding forward, pushed past James, elbowed Mandy aside and bolted the door shut again.

'We don't use that stall, and there's nothing in it for you to see,' he said, staring at them both suspiciously. 'What are you doing poking around in here anyway?'

'I'm sorry,' Mandy stammered. 'I was just wondering whose stall it was, and . . .' Her voice trailed away lamely.

'We've come with Mr Hope, the relief vet,' James said, taking over. 'Mr Johnson said we could have a look round, but we didn't mean to cause trouble. Can we give you a hand with anything?'

'Yes, we'd like to help,' said Mandy, shooting James a grateful look. 'Just tell us what needs doing. You must have a lot of work around here.'

'That's true enough,' Tom admitted. He stared at them both, trying to make up his mind. 'With the vet, you said?'

'Yes,' said Mandy quickly. 'He's my father. I'm Mandy Hope, by the way – and this is my friend, James Hunter.'

James nodded and smiled.

'All right then,' Tom said eventually. 'You can do some mucking out, if you're so keen. The other two lads have taken a couple of horses out on the gallops, so I could do with the help. Take the barrow and start off with Double-Decker's stall, and I'll tell you which ones to clean after that, if you're still on your feet. Just keep away from this one, OK? We don't use it.'

He took up the wheelbarrow again and James and Mandy followed him across the aisle to Double-Decker's stable.

'Hello there, gorgeous,' he said, clicking his tongue as he unbolted the door and went in. Double-Decker was a rangy-looking strawberry roan who started back apprehensively as he approached her. 'Now then, silly girl,' he said soothingly. 'You know me!'

Tom took a headcollar down from the wall and slipped it over the mare's head, attaching a lead rope to it, then carefully brought her out of the stall. 'One of the stars of the show, she is,' he said proudly. 'She can run like the wind.'

Mandy and James stood back as the horse came by, not wanting to alarm her.

When she was safely tethered to a ring on the wall, Mandy came slowly nearer, making sure Double-Decker could see her clearly and could tell that she wasn't a threat. Talking softly to her, Mandy then stretched out a cautious hand and rubbed the mare's velvety nose. 'We'll get your stall nice and clean, I promise,' she said.

'Thanks,' Tom said gruffly. 'Know what to do, do you?' Mandy nodded, and he went on, 'Well, I won't be far away – just give me a shout if you're not sure about anything.'

Mandy and James worked in silence, tipping all the droppings into the wheelbarrow, then separating the clean and dirty bedding. Queenie curled herself in a heap of straw in a corner of the stall, and Double-Decker dozed off where she stood.

'Glad to see you're being useful!' called Mr Hope with a grin as he came back into the barn with Harry Johnson. They began to examine another of the horses, and were soon deep in conversation.

'Well, I think we're nearly done here,' Mandy said at last, leaning on her pitchfork and blowing her hair out of her eyes. 'Hard work, isn't it?'

'Phew! Sure is!' James replied. He straightened up and looked down the aisle at all the other stalls, some still waiting to be cleaned out. 'I can see why they've got behind here, if there's only three stable lads to clean out all these stalls – along with all their other jobs!' he said.

Mandy nodded. 'Mr Johnson did say they were short-staffed at the moment, though,' she reminded him. 'I'll just get the wheelbarrow.'

Together they piled all the dirty straw into the barrow, then spread out the fresh bedding. At last, they both looked over the clean and tidy stall, satisfied with their work.

Footsteps echoed down the barn, and Tom put his head round the doorway. 'Good job,' he said approvingly. 'Done that before, have you?'

James nodded. 'We know someone with a pony, and we help her occasionally.' Their friend, Susan Collins, was always glad of a hand looking after her chestnut pony, Prince.

'Well, if you've still got the energy, there are a couple more stalls that could do with the same treatment,' Tom said. 'That'll give the horses a nice surprise when they come back from the gallops. Not to mention the lads!'

He smiled at James and Mandy. 'I reckon we'll all owe you a favour after this,' he said, untying Double-Decker. 'Come on, girl, back into your nice clean bedroom.'

The mare sailed gracefully in and immediately took a long drink from her freshly filled water bucket.

'I think she approves,' Tom said as he bolted the door behind her. He grasped the wheelbarrow handles. 'Follow me and I'll show you these stalls. I'll do one and you can do the other. And I'll even take this load to the muckheap for you.'

'You're too kind,' Mandy teased. She could tell Tom had decided they were OK.

'D'you two want a job here?' Harry Johnson asked as they walked past. 'You're good workers!'

'Oh, they're used to hard labour,' Mr Hope said, looking round from a fine black horse whose teeth he was examining. 'We train them up well at Animal Ark.'

James and Mandy forked and swept and raked until their backs were aching. They could hear a background murmur of voices as the two men worked their way down the rows of stalls, looking at each of the horses inside. Mandy made out phrases like 'pipe-opener on the gallops' and 'born on the bit', along with other technical terms she couldn't make head nor tail of.

Eventually Mr Hope put his head over the

stall door and said, 'Harry and I are pretty well finished here – we're just going to have a chat in the office. Do you two want to join us down there when you're ready?'

'OK, Dad,' Mandy replied. 'We won't be too much longer.'

In another ten minutes or so, their second stall was looking spotless and James had taken the dirty straw out to the muckheap. 'I'll tell Tom we've finished,' he said as he returned with the empty barrow. 'I think we've done our bit, don't you?'

'Absolutely,' Mandy agreed. 'And I could do with a drink.'

'Thanks a lot,' Tom said, after he'd seen the results of their hard work. 'That's a big help. I've only got one more to do now.' He grinned at their tired, dirty faces. 'Not much fun mucking out, is it? Riding's the best part – that's what I'm here for. I want to be a jockey, like Jim and Pete.'

'Do you ride the horses here?' Mandy asked. 'That must be fantastic!'

'I do when I get the chance,' Tom muttered, leaning against the stall door. 'All the stable lads do – but as there's only the three of us now we seem to spend most of our time shovelling muck, grooming and cleaning tack from dawn till dusk.'

Mandy hesitated. Tom seemed so much more friendly now. Maybe he'd answer some of their questions. She looked across at James and he gave her an encouraging nod that seemed to say, 'Go on – it's worth a try.'

'Tom, do the horses seem a bit – well, unsettled to you?' she asked carefully.

Tom sighed. He unbolted a stall door on the other side of them and led out its inhabitant, a nervous-looking piebald, tethering him to a wall ring. Then, as he began to pile the dirty straw from the stall into a wheelbarrow, he began to talk.

'They are off-form, and that's a fact,' he admitted. 'Wasn't always like this, though,' he continued. 'When I came here end of last year, Folan's was a different place. Then a lot of things happened, one after the other. Old Mr Folan died and his son took over. That was all right, to begin with. But before long, everything started to go wrong . . .' He picked up the handles of the now-full barrow to wheel it outside.

'Why?' Mandy prompted gently. 'What started it all?'

Tom hesitated, then put the barrow down again. 'There was an accident a couple of months ago,' he said at last. 'One of the horses had to be put down.'

'Oh, how awful!' Mandy exclaimed. 'What happened?' She and James watched as Tom searched for the right words.

'He got injured on the racecourse. Had to be destroyed, there and then,' Tom explained. 'That's the bare bones of it, anyway. Probably the finest horse we've ever had here, and it hit us all very hard – especially young Mr Folan. He was riding him at the time, you see . . . The life just seemed to go out of this place after that.'

Tom picked up the barrow handles again, seeming anxious to be off. Perhaps he felt he'd said too much, Mandy thought.

'Shouldn't you two get down to the office?' he said. 'Your dad'll be wondering where you are.' Then he hurried out of the barn.

'What a terrible thing to happen,' James said.

'It seems such an awful waste,' Mandy added. 'I can hardly bear to think about it – a beautiful animal losing its life, just for sport.' Her eyes filled with tears.

James nodded. 'But racing's what these animals are bred for, Mandy,' he said. 'I bet they have a fantastic life. And I think accidents like that are very rare.' He linked his arm though hers. 'Come on, let's see if Mr Johnson will give us a drink. I reckon we've earned it! Look, Queenie is waiting for us.' The terrier was sitting near the barn entrance, looking expectantly at them.

'OK,' said Mandy, blowing her nose. She knew James was trying to cheer her up, but it seemed such a sad story: a beautiful horse having to be put down, and the whole stables so affected by his death.

As she followed James along the central passageway, Mandy suddenly stopped. Something made her turn around to look back. Her eyes were drawn to the unused stall as if by an irresistible magnetic force. 'Come on, James,' she said. 'We've got to go and have a look inside that stall. It might be our last chance!'

'But Tom told us to keep out of there!' James said anxiously. 'Do you think we can risk it?'

'You'll have to keep a look-out,' Mandy replied, 'and tell me when he's coming back. Can you see where he is now?'

'He's almost reached the muckheap, I think,' James answered, narrowing his eyes as he stared out of the barn. 'OK – if we're going to do it we'd better be quick!'

Together they hurried back to the unused stall. Seeing where they were heading, Queenie scampered over to them, growling unhappily at their ankles as they approached the stall.

James tried to quieten the little dog down and, as quickly as she could, Mandy drew back the bolt and slipped inside.

The air in the stall seemed much colder than outside. Mandy shivered, then shook her head. That was silly, it couldn't be – could it? She hugged her arms over her chest, her teeth chattering, and gazed around, uncertain what she was expecting to find.

'Can you see anything?' James asked in an urgent whisper.

'No, nothing,' she replied, scanning the bare concrete walls. A faint sighing, like a gentle breeze, was all she could hear. And then, suddenly, a freezing breath blew gently on the back of Mandy's neck.

Mandy gasped in shock. She had felt the breath quite distinctly. Yet, somehow, she knew that she was in no danger. She turned slowly round – but there was nothing there.

'Mandy!' James whispered, his anxious face peering at her over the door of the stall. 'Tom's coming! Get out of there!'

There was no time to think. Quickly, Mandy turned towards the door – and then stopped short. Hanging on a hook in the corner was a headcollar. She hadn't noticed it at first. She lifted it off the hook and ran her fingers over the worn leather. It was so cold! Like everything else about this stable.

'What are you doing? He'll catch you!' James hissed, hopping up and down frantically.

'OK. Coming,' she answered and hastily jammed the collar back on its hook. Out of the corner of her eye she saw something gleam as it fell from the collar and landed on the ground with a faint tinkle. Mandy snatched it up. It was a strip of engraved metal, which she thrust into a pocket as she slipped out of the stall and rammed the bolt home.

Not a moment too soon. Tom was coming towards them, pushing the barrow.

'Just saying goodbye to Hadrian!' Mandy said as casually as she could, and he nodded to them. He didn't seem to have noticed anything.

'Phew, that was a close one,' said James, when they were out of earshot. 'I thought my heart would stop beating! Did you find anything?'

'Only this,' Mandy said, pulling the strip of metal out of her pocket.'It fell off as I was putting the headcollar back.' By now they were out of the barn and she held the strip of brass up to the bright daylight to examine the engraving on it.

'What is it?' James asked.

'A nameplate, I think,' Mandy said, squinting at the writing. 'Look, it's got the word "Tibor" engraved on it.' She passed the thin strip of metal over to James and watched as he examined it too.

'Tibor must have been the horse who had that stall,' he said. 'Do you think he could be—'

'—the one who had to be put down?' Mandy finished off for him. 'Yes, I'm sure of it,' she said. 'And do you know what, James?' Mandy took a deep breath. 'I think he was there, just now, in the stable. I felt something in there with me. I know I did!'

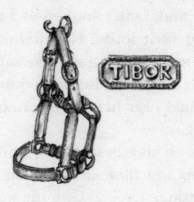

Four

James looked at Mandy, wide-eyed, but there was no time to say any more as they had arrived outside the office. Queenie trotted boldly through the open office door, but James held Mandy back as an angry voice came sounding out.

'I tell you, Harry, I'm not happy about the way things are going, and it's not just because I've been bucked off – again!' said the voice. 'I've been telling you for weeks the horses aren't right, and no one seems to be doing a thing about it. Well, now even *I* have had enough!'

Mandy and James looked at each other, wondering what to do. Now didn't seem the best time to go bursting into the office. There was clearly a heated discussion going on, and Mandy could hear her father's voice amongst the others.

'Let's wait out here for a while,' James whispered, and they sat down on a wooden bench outside.

Harry Johnson's voice rose above the others. 'I've told you we're doing all we can, Pete,' they heard him say. 'We've got Mr Hope here now, for one thing.'

'Well, let's hope he's a miracle worker,' came the grumpy reply, 'because he needs to be. If we can't break this run of bad luck, Folan's is going to go under. And me and Jim are not going down with it, that's for certain.'

With that, the door was flung open, and two men came storming out. They paid no attention to Mandy and James, sitting quietly on the bench.

'They must be the jockeys here,' James said to Mandy as they watched the men head off towards the red van. 'I recognised one of them

– he went off in that van after Hadrian bolted.'

'So the other one must be Hadrian's rider, who was thrown,' Mandy said. 'Well, I'm glad he's all right, but he certainly sounds furious! Let's give it another few minutes and then go in and see what's happening.'

A little while later, she knocked on the office door and then opened it quietly. Adam Hope and Harry Johnson were deep in conversation, sitting either side of a large desk covered in papers.

'Oh, hello there, you two,' said her father, turning round.

'Sorry, Dad, are we interrupting you?' Mandy asked.

'No, don't worry,' said Harry Johnson, pulling out a couple of chairs and beckoning to them to sit down. 'We won't be a minute. We're pretty well finished, aren't we?' He looked appealingly at Mr Hope.

'More or less,' Mr Hope replied.

Mandy and James sat down as quietly as they could. Mandy watched the stable manager. He still looked rather nervous to her – perhaps he was worried that her father would wash his hands of Folan's too.

'But, as I told you, I really do need to see Mr Folan,' Mr Hope continued firmly. 'We've got to talk to him about hiring some extra staff. You can see how fed up your jockeys are, and the stable lads you have left have far too much to do.'

'I know, I know,' said Harry Johnson, fiddling with a couple of paperclips on his desk. 'It's just such a problem getting hold of him.'

'But he's the owner of the yard!' said Mr Hope. 'Surely he can see how important this is? Your horses won't stand a chance if they're not properly looked after and exercised. Can't he afford to have more people working here?'

'It's not a question of money,' Mr Johnson replied. He threw the paperclips down on the desk and looked Mr Hope full in the face, as though finally making up his mind to confide in him. 'He's lost interest in the place, that's what's happened.'

'But the horses are depending on him!' Mandy blurted out, unable to stop herself. 'He can't just give up on them!'

Harry Johnson sighed heavily. 'It's a bit more

complicated than that,' he said quietly.

Mandy leaned forward. 'Is it something to do with the accident?' she asked without thinking. James shot her a warning look, but it was too late now.

'Oh, so you know about that, do you?' Mr Johnson said, giving her a keen look. 'Been talking to Tom, have you? What did he say?'

'Just that one of the horses got injured on the racetrack and had to be put down,' James answered.

'He didn't really want to talk about it,' Mandy added, not wanting to get Tom into trouble for saying things he shouldn't have.

'No, well, everybody took it very badly,' Mr Johnson said, pushing his chair back and getting to his feet. 'Young Mr Folan, in particular. There was rather more to it than that, you see.' He paused, staring out of the window with his hands in his pockets and a faraway expression on his face.

Long, silent seconds went by. 'Go on,' said Mr Hope, curiously.

Mr Johnson turned back to look at them, rather surprised, as though he'd forgotten they were there for a moment. He shook his head. 'Sorry,' he said. Then, clearing his throat, he began. 'Mr Folan was riding the horse when it happened. He was a marvellous animal, but he needed careful handling. The jockey who was going to ride him had fallen in a race earlier on, so Mr Folan took his place.'

'Was he allowed to?' asked James. 'Don't you need a licence to take part in a race like that?'

'Oh, he'd been passed by the Jockey Club a couple of months before,' Mr Johnson replied. 'He didn't have the experience, though, and he was on the heavy side as well. We all tried to tell him not to do it, but he wouldn't listen to any of us.' The stable manager shook his head sadly. 'No, he wouldn't be told, insisted on riding. And look what happened . . .'

'Tom didn't really give us any details,' James said, prompting the stable manager to carry on.

'Well, it was a flat race – no jumps,' Mr Johnson continued, sitting back down again. 'The runners were bunched very close together. Young Mr Folan tried to break through a gap in the field that wasn't there. Somehow, his horse stumbled – and got kicked full in the face by the horse ahead . . .'

'Oh, how terrible!' Mandy gasped, her hand flying up to her face in shock.

'It was an awful injury,' Mr Johnson said, shaking his head. 'The kindest thing to do was to put the creature out of his misery.'

'I can see an accident like that wouldn't be easy to get over,' Mr Hope said gravely. 'I've put down some badly-hurt animals in my time, and it's not something you ever forget.'

Mr Johnson nodded in agreement. 'Everyone hates it when a horse has to be destroyed,' he said, 'but young Mr Folan felt it was all his fault. And Tibor was so special, it just made everything worse. Our head lad left a month later – he couldn't stand being here any more.'

'Tibor,' repeated Mandy, looking at James and turning over the nameplate in her pocket.

'Yes, Tibor, that was his name,' said Mr Johnson. 'He was a wonderful horse, and he could run like the wind. Quite highly-strung, but gentle as a lamb in the right hands. I've got a picture of him somewhere.' He began to rifle through one of the desk drawers, pulling out a sheaf of papers. 'Mr Folan ordered us to get rid of everything to do with him – we even had to take the nameplate off his stall. I kept one particular photograph, though. Couldn't bear to throw it away.'

'So he blames himself for Tibor's death,' said Mr Hope. 'But can't he see there are other horses here who need his attention?'

Mr Johnson shook his head. 'He just can't bear to come near the place. I've got to admit it, the last vet we had here wouldn't put up with it any more – that's why he left. Mr Folan just wouldn't talk to him. He'll see me once a week or so if I really push it, but he won't have anything to do with anybody else.'

'Then perhaps Mr Folan should consider selling the stables,' Mr Hope said seriously.

Mr Johnson shook his head. 'He can't bring himself to do that either. It's been a family business for years. But we can't go on like this much longer. I'm at my wits' end.'

He stopped searching through a bulging file of papers and looked at Mr Hope with a shamefaced expression. 'I should have told you all this in the beginning, I know, but I didn't want to put you off working here. Still, in a way I'm glad you know everything now. Oh, help!' He made a vain grab at the file as it slid off his lap and all the papers inside cascaded to the ground.

'Here's a photograph,' Mandy said, spotting the corner of a black-and-white print amongst the pile. Dropping to her knees, she pulled it out – then drew in her breath. The photograph showed a magnificent stallion. Its coat was a dazzling silvery-white – though Mandy knew that, in equine terms, it would be described as 'grey'. His mane and tail rippled like white silk.

Mandy passed the photograph up to Harry Johnson. 'Is this the one you were looking for?' she asked.

'Yes, that's the one. That's Tibor,' said Mr Johnson sadly, taking a look at the picture and then tossing it down on the desk. 'We'll never see another horse like that here. One in a million, he was.'

James gave his glasses a quick polish and picked up the photograph. 'Look at the size of him!' he breathed.

Mandy peered over his shoulder. There was

something very familiar about that horse. She was sure she'd seen him before. But how? And where?

Mr Hope craned forward for a look, too. 'He's superb,' he agreed. 'Lovely deep chest, and see how proudly he holds his head!'

He must have been looking towards the person taking the photograph when it was taken, as he seemed to be staring straight out of the picture with his dark, soulful eyes.

'I've got it!' Mandy said, looking up at Harry Johnson. 'I was trying to remember which horse Tibor reminds me of and it's just come to me – he looks very like a horse I saw in one of your fields this morning!'

'What horse in what field?' said Mr Johnson, puzzled.

'The grey, in the field by the turning up to the stables. The one I told you about, James!' Mandy said, turning to him. 'I saw him clearly! He was looking straight at me, just like Tibor's doing in this picture.'

'That's impossible,' Mr Johnson said, staring at her. 'We don't have a grey at Folan's any longer. Tibor was the only one, and you can be sure Mr Folan won't take on another.'

'But I saw him, I really did!' Mandy repeated. 'I wasn't dreaming – I even took a photo!'

'You couldn't have done,' said Mr Johnson shortly, losing patience. He pushed back his chair and stood up abruptly. 'I told you, there's no grey at Folan's!' he said sharply, walking over to the office door and holding it open. 'Not any more.'

There was an awkward pause. 'Oh well,

perhaps you've got in a muddle, Mandy,' said her father, collecting his notes and his bag and getting up too. 'We must be on our way, Harry. Thanks for showing me around. I'll be in touch as soon as I can with the results of those blood tests.'

Mandy felt herself blushing as she and James followed her father to the door. Why was Mr Johnson getting so angry? She was only describing what she'd seen, yet he seemed to be reacting as though she were playing some kind of tasteless joke.

'Look, I didn't mean to bite your head off,' the stable manager said gruffly, seeing her hurt expression. 'We all make mistakes. I know what, how would you like some tickets for the races next Saturday? We've got a couple of horses running – maybe you'll bring them luck. We could do with it, I tell you! Our last few races have been a disaster.'

'Oh, Dad, can we?' Mandy asked, feeling a little better. 'Please? That would be great!'

James nodded enthusiastically. 'I'm staying with you next weekend while Mum and Dad are away, remember?'

'Well,' said Mr Hope, hesitantly. 'It sounds good to me, but we'd better check what's happening at Animal Ark on that day before we accept the invitation.'

'I could get you into the Members' enclosure,' Harry Johnson told him with a significant look. 'You might just catch young Mr Folan there. He did tell me he was planning on going, though I'll believe it when I see it. He hasn't been near a racecourse since the accident.'

'In that case, I think we should make it a date,' Mr Hope replied firmly, as they shook hands. 'I've got a few things to say to your "young Mr Folan", and I hope he's going to listen!'

Five

'I tell you, James, I really felt as though someone – or something – was in Tibor's stall with me,' said Mandy, filling up a clean water bottle and hooking it back in the rabbit's cage. 'That's the only way I can describe it. There was a chilly breath on the back of my neck.'

It had been such a busy week at school that they'd hardly had a chance to talk over the happenings at Folan's the previous weekend. But now it was Saturday morning again and James had arrived to stay while his parents went off on a business trip. School was forgotten for the time being – all they could think about were the stables, and how the horses would race that afternoon.

James sat stroking the soft fur of a huge lop-eared rabbit, deep in thought. 'So, let me get this right,' he said, eventually. 'You're saying that you think Tibor's presence is still there at Folan's – and that's what's making the other horses so nervous?'

Mandy nodded. 'You felt how strange and chilly it was in that barn, didn't you? And it's not a virus that's making the horses so unsettled. Dad thought it might have been, but he got the blood tests back yesterday and all the horses are clear.'

She filled the dropper from a small bottle of eyedrops. 'Can you just keep Dylan's head still for me while I put in his drops, please, James?' she asked. 'He looks so comfortable on your lap.'

'His eyes must be really sore,' James said sympathetically as Mandy carefully squeezed in the drops. 'He can hardly open them!'

'I know,' Mandy replied. 'But it's amazing how quickly the antibiotics work. Mum said she thinks he'll only need to spend another night in here.' She lifted the rabbit up and put him carefully back in his clean cage, shutting the door securely.

'Well, something's definitely put the horses off form, we know that,' James went on, tickling the rabbit's nose through the wire mesh. 'Your theory sounds a bit crazy, but maybe you're right. There's definitely *something* strange going on at Folan's, what with those storms Mr Johnson was telling us about, and that grey stallion you saw in the field that shouldn't have been there.'

'Yes, that's another thing!' Mandy said excitedly, washing her hands again. 'I *did* see that horse, as clearly as anything, yet Mr Johnson insisted that they no longer have a grey at Folan's.'

'Well, when you get those photos back we can show him,' James said. 'Maybe he'll recognise the horse when he sees it, and the mystery will be solved.' He made for the door. 'Come on, let's go and see what Blackie's up to in the kitchen.'

James's black Labrador was staying the

weekend too, and he'd been shut up out of harm's way while Mrs Hope took Saturday morning surgery.

'Hello there, you two.' Mr Hope looked up from a pile of sandwiches on the bread board as they came into the kitchen. 'Done all the chores?'

'Yup, we've cleaned out all the cages and given Dylan his drops,' Mandy said, bending down to give the excitable Labrador a stroke. 'Hello there, boy! Have you been getting in the way?'

'He's been watching me like a hawk,' Mr Hope smiled. 'I think he's wondering how much of the picnic he's going to be eating.'

'We can take him with us, can't we?' James asked, as Blackie looked up eagerly at him.

'Yes, I think so,' Mr Hope said. 'We probably won't be able to take him on to the racecourse, but we can leave him in the Land-rover with the windows open, and give him a run round the carpark. Oh, Mandy – here's something for you,' he said, wiping his hands on a tea towel and taking a brightly coloured wallet out of his jacket pocket. 'I got your photos back from the chemist yesterday and promptly forgot all about them.'

'Oh, thanks!' Mandy said as her father passed over the envelope. She tore it open and began flicking hurriedly through the prints to find the one she'd taken of the grey stallion. Once they'd seen the photograph, everyone would have to believe there had been a stallion very like Tibor in that field.

Coming to the first of the photographs she had taken on the visit to Folan's, Mandy found herself looking at a photograph of a green field. There was a dark wood behind it and a sturdy fence in front. But not a horse in sight.

Mandy stared down at the photograph in disbelief. 'There must be some mistake!' she muttered, leafing through the remaining prints. Pictures of the horses inside the shadowy barn had come out even more clearly than she had hoped. She looked back again at the picture of the empty field.

'What is it?' asked James, seeing her shocked face.

'I don't believe it!' Mandy exclaimed, still staring at the print. 'That's impossible! I saw the horse – he was right in the middle of the viewfinder!' She felt as though an icy hand was squeezing her insides. What was going on?

'What's the matter, love?' said her father. 'You've gone as white as a sheet.'

'That grey stallion I took a photograph of,' Mandy said slowly, holding out the print of the empty field. 'He's not here. He's disappeared.'

'He must have moved out of the frame just as you pressed the shutter release,' James said as they sped along in the Land-rover.

'No, he didn't. He was standing still, staring straight at me as I took the photograph,' Mandy insisted. 'I remember it clearly!' She had gone over and over the scene in her mind, without coming any closer to an answer. The horse *had* been there. She *had* taken a photograph of him. So why hadn't he come out on the print? It was as if he'd vanished into thin air.

'Look, Mandy,' said her father, turning round from the front passenger seat, 'there's got to be some explanation and, whatever it is, you'll find out sooner or later. Just forget about the whole thing for the moment. We're off to the races now – don't spoil the day by fretting over mysteries you can't solve.'

'OK, Dad,' Mandy sighed. 'I'll put it to the back of my mind – for now.' She was tired of going round in circles. Blackie gave a low whine from the back, and she put her hand through the grille and stroked one of his silky ears.

'That's the way,' her mother said encouragingly, adjusting the driving mirror so she could give Mandy a quick look. 'Now, I know what'll help take your mind off things. You and James can each choose a favourite for every race, and the one with the most winners gets to choose what we watch on TV tonight!'

By now, the traffic was beginning to thicken up, and soon they were turning into the crowded racecourse carpark.

Mrs Hope was guided to a space by a bowler-hatted attendant, in between a Mercedes and a Rolls-Royce. 'Better be careful how I go!' she grinned. 'Don't want to scratch either of those.'

'The tickets should be waiting for us at the gate,' said Mr Hope. 'Harry said he'd leave them for us to pick up. Why don't we see what's going on and then come back here in an hour or so to have our picnic? We can give Blackie a quick run afterwards,' he said, smiling at James.

'Great, Dad,' said Mandy, already scrambling out of the Land-rover. 'Now let's get going!'

Once through the entrance gate and in the raceground itself, Mandy and James gasped in amazement. There were so many people! Crowds milled around the rails along the racetrack and filled the stands overlooking it.

Expensively dressed women, dripping with jewellery, rubbed shoulders with bandy-legged men in threadbare tweed jackets. Now and then a jockey in colourful silks and white breeches strode purposefully along. Everyone was busy looking at newspapers and racecards, scanning the field with binoculars, or talking together over Thermos flasks and shooting sticks.

'What's that man doing?' James asked Mr Hope, looking at someone flapping his hands in a kind of complicated sign language.

'Oh, he's a tic-tac man, a kind of bookie,' Mr Hope replied. 'He's indicating what the odds are, for people who want to place last-minute bets. So they know how much money they'll get if their horse wins.'

A race was already in progress, horses thundering round the track.

'Come on, James!' Mandy said, pulling at his sleeve. 'Let's go nearer the track to get a better view.'

'Why don't we all meet up at the paddock when the race is over? It's just there,' Mrs Hope suggested, pointing to a ring circled round with a white fence. 'That's where they parade the horses before they start, so everyone can get a look at them.'

'Yes, that'll give me time to see if I can find anyone from Folan's,' Mr Hope said, scanning the crowd. 'Here, take a racecard so you know what's going on.'

'Thanks, Dad,' Mandy said. 'We'll see you after the race!'

'This is wonderful, isn't it?' James said to her, his eyes shining as they hurried along towards the track. 'There's so much going on!'

They found a good spot by the railings and waited for the horses to gallop by. A few voices in the crowd were cheering, and an excited commentary blared out over the loudspeaker system.

'I can't hear myself think!' Mandy shouted, her hands over her ears, as the leaders approached. The pounding of hooves became deafening and the ground seemed to tremble beneath her feet. Most of the horses were bunched fairly closely together, but a dappled grey and a chestnut were well out in front.

Close to where James and Mandy were standing was a fence the horses had to jump. They both gasped in awe when, right in front of them, the two leading horses took off, soaring into the air and over it. Divots of mud and grass flew up as they landed on the other side. The jockeys shouted encouragement as they urged their mounts on.

In a matter of seconds, the rest of the competitors were up and over the jump, and then they had all gone, taking the noise and fury with them.

'Wow!' said James. 'That was incredible! I never realised how high the jumps were. You wouldn't think the horses could possibly get over them!'

'I wonder who's winning,' Mandy said, gazing after the horses. 'Why don't we go to the finishing line and see what's happening?'

The next minute, there was a smattering of applause and people flooded on to the race track. As they came closer, they could see the jockey on the dappled grey bending down to shake as many of the hands reaching up to him as he could. Then he was led off through the crowd on his sweating horse.

'They'll be taking him to the winners' enclosure,' Mandy said. 'I wonder if any of Folan's horses will be going there today?'

James was looking at the racecard and checking his watch. 'Double-Decker's running in the next race!' he said. 'Do you remember? We cleaned out her stall. Come on, let's get over to the paddock and see how she looks.'

They made their way over and soon found Mandy's parents, leaning on the rails and watching a string of long-legged thoroughbreds being led around the ring.

'Did you find Mr Johnson?' Mandy asked her father.

'No, I couldn't see him anywhere,' he replied. 'There's Tom, though, opposite us. Looks like he's got his hands full with that roan.'

'Oh, come on, Double-Decker!' Mandy groaned as she looked across. 'That's not the way to behave!'

Tom was struggling to control the mare. She looked twice as jumpy as she had in the barn, and seemed determined not to walk in the same direction as the others. In fact, she didn't seem to want to go anywhere at all. She snorted, rolling her eyes and dancing backwards so that she nearly cannoned into the horses behind.

'Poor Tom,' said James. 'It must be awful, trying to lead her on in front of all these people staring at him.'

'You say all the horses at Folan's are off form at the moment, Adam?' Mrs Hope asked her husband curiously. 'And there seems to be no physical reason for it?'

'That's about the size of it,' Mr Hope agreed. 'Harry said none of the horses have been placed in a race for the past couple of months.' Mr Hope scratched his beard, perplexed. 'I thought at first that some kind of virus might have been to blame,' he continued. 'But the blood tests were all clear. I don't know what the problem is – yet.'

Just then, a signal was given for the jockeys to mount. A man wearing blue-and-yellow colours walked towards Double-Decker.

Mandy nudged James. 'Isn't that one of the riders we saw at Folan's?' she asked.

'Yes, he's the one who got thrown. Pete, I think his name was,' James replied. 'I wonder how he'll get on today?'

The jockey leaped nimbly up into the saddle, but Double-Decker was still reluctant to walk on, no matter how hard the man squeezed her sides. Eventually he lost patience and gave the horse a smart tap with his whip. Double-Decker began to buck, kicking up her heels. With a muttered curse, her rider slid to the ground and led her out of the ring to try to calm her down, Tom following beside him.

A murmur ran round the crowd of people watching and Mandy caught her father's eye. He gave her a quick shrug of the shoulders. It wasn't a promising start to the race.

The other horses went to line up at the starting tape, and Mandy lost sight of Double-Decker for a moment. As she searched for the jockey's blue-and-yellow silks in the orderly row, the riders suddenly scattered in several different directions. At the centre of the confusion was Double-Decker, rearing and kicking, lashing out at everything around her.

'That's Double-Decker! What *is* she doing?' James cried, clutching Mandy's arm.

'She'll never be able to race after this,' Mandy said anxiously. 'Dad, isn't there anything we can do?'

But it was too late. A steward shouted through a megaphone, 'Keep that horse well back!' and then, seconds later, an announcement came over the loudspeaker system. 'Horse number four, Double-Decker, has been withdrawn from the race.'

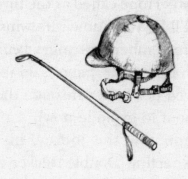

Six

Mandy and James looked at each other in alarm at the news.

'That's terrible!' Mandy said. 'She's not even had the chance to run.'

'I think I'd better get over there,' Mr Hope said. 'She might have hurt herself. I should help check her over.'

'Can we come too?' Mandy asked.

'OK, but I'd keep in the background if I were you,' Mr Hope replied. 'I should think tempers might be running high.'

'See you back at the car when this race has

finished,' Mrs Hope called as the three of them went off. 'I'll let you know who wins!'

'Do you remember how angry Pete was when we saw him last week?' James said to Mandy as they followed her father through the crowd. 'I bet he's about to explode now!'

They soon saw the jockey, his face like thunder, wheeling Double-Decker away from the starting line. The horse was pirouetting and dancing backwards, showing the whites of her eyes and snorting. When they were well away from the other horses, the man dismounted.

'Oh look, there's Tom!' Mandy said to James, as the stable lad came hurrying up to take the reins.

'Get this stupid animal out of my sight!' they heard the jockey say furiously as he handed her over. 'This is the last time I'm riding for Folan's, I can tell you that. Folan's jockeys have become the laughing-stock of the changing room!' And he stormed off in disgust.

Tom nodded a greeting as James and Mandy came up with Mr Hope.

'Bad luck, Tom,' said Mandy sympathetically. 'We really felt for you there in the paddock.'

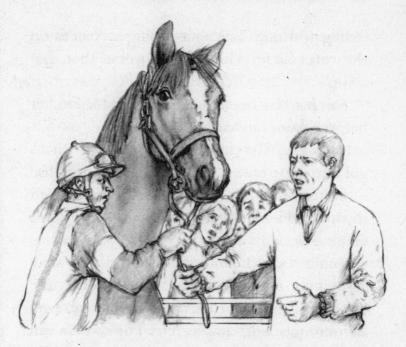

'Oh, I'm getting used to it,' he replied tersely, concentrating on getting Double-Decker to stand quietly.

'Have you got any idea what unsettled her just now?' Mr Hope asked, beginning to look the mare over while Mandy and James stood beside Tom at her head.

'Not a clue,' Tom replied. 'She's been running OK on the gallops. You might find something I've missed, but I don't think there's much really wrong with her. She's just going to pieces on the racecourse. This is even worse than last time!'

'So this has happened with Double-Decker before?' James asked.

' 'Fraid so,' Tom said. 'I just don't know what's got into these horses over the past few months.'

'I must say, I didn't realise things were as bad as this,' said Mr Hope, running a hand down Double-Decker's legs.

Tom sighed. 'I can't understand it,' he said, scratching the mare's nose. 'The horses are jumpy enough in the barn, but we just can't get them to race – it's impossible! The owners will start to take them away from the yard, and I'd do the same in their shoes.'

'Have you talked to Mr Folan about it?' Mandy asked.

Tom gave a short laugh. 'We never see him these days,' he said, 'let alone talk to him. You'd think he'd be here today, wouldn't you, but there's no sign of him. Mr Johnson went off to look for him a while ago and I haven't seen him since.'

'I was hoping to talk to him,' Mr Hope said,

straightening up. 'He really needs some more staff up at the yard, though I'm sure I don't need to tell you that.'

'No, you don't!' Tom said, with feeling. 'Me and the other two lads are worked off our feet, and there's hardly enough riders now for all the horses we've got. If Pete goes, I don't know what we'll do.'

'Well, let's try and look on the bright side,' said Mr Hope, giving Double-Decker a pat. 'I can't find much seriously wrong with your mare – after a quick look, anyway. You'd better take her back to the holding yard. The course vet will probably want to take a blood sample and run a dope test.'

'And the races aren't over yet,' James said. 'Have you got any other horses running?'

'Pilgrim's Progress is in the two-thirty,' Tom replied. 'Did you meet him up at the stables last week?'

'Yes!' said Mandy, brightening up. 'He's that lovely bay, isn't he? Maybe he'll save the day. What do you think his chances are?'

'Oh, none of the others can touch him when he's on form,' Tom replied, smiling a little. 'He could run the socks off any of them here, and Jim always used to get the best out of him. But who knows how he'll run now?' Lowering his voice, he added, 'These days, I wouldn't bet on any of the horses at Folan's.'

Mr Hope gave Tom a sympathetic pat on the shoulder then turned to Mandy and James. 'Well, we must be getting back,' he said. 'There's a picnic waiting for us. Goodbye, Tom, and good luck!'

'We'll be cheering for Pilgrim!' Mandy added, as Tom led Double-Decker off to the yard where the horses were kept before and after a race.

'Thanks,' Tom called back over his shoulder. 'Let's hope he can hear you!'

'I feel sorry for Tom,' James said as they walked over to the Land-rover. 'I bet he gets a lot of the blame when things go wrong, and it's not really his fault.'

'No,' said Mr Hope. 'It can't be much fun for any of them at Folan's right now. They must all be very worried. Once the owners start taking their horses away, the yard's finished. That's probably why Mr Johnson wanted to keep quiet about the problems they'd been having. Rumours spread like wildfire in this business.'

'It's not the horses' fault, though, either,' Mandy said. 'It's not like they're playing up on purpose. Something must be the matter with them, Dad, and Mr Folan ought to be helping you to find out what it is!'

Mr Hope didn't answer directly. He was shading his eyes with one hand and looking over towards the Animal Ark Land-rover in the middle of the carpark. 'What's going on there?' he said. 'I think something's happened . . .'

Mandy and James looked. Emily Hope was standing with her hands on her hips and a frown on her face.

'Oh dear,' James said anxiously. 'Perhaps it's Blackie!' And he began to run.

'Wait for me!' Mandy called, sprinting after him.

'Is it Blackie?' they asked in unison, as they arrived, panting. Mr Hope followed a few seconds behind, and leaned against the side of the Land-rover to get his breath back.

'Yes, it certainly *is* Blackie,' said Mrs Hope, sternly. The Labrador was cowering at her feet, tail between his legs, looking up at her sorrowfully.

'Take a look in the back of the Land-rover,' Mrs Hope went on.

'Oh no!' James gasped, looking through the car window. 'The picnic!'

The remains of the picnic were littered all over the back seat. Blackie had had a feast: empty crisp packets, chicken bones, a few shreds of silver foil and some greaseproof paper were all that was left.

'I don't believe it!' groaned Mr Hope. 'All my carefully made sandwiches!'

'Do you realise what that dog has eaten?' said Mrs Hope. 'Half a dozen vegetarian sausages, a mountain of cheese sandwiches, half a cold chicken and a whole fruitcake that Gran made yesterday. *And* he's chewed up a large part of the picnic hamper for good measure.'

'Oh, Blackie!' James said, horrified. 'I'm really sorry, everyone. Blackie! How could you?'

Blackie sank down to the ground and put his head on his front paws, twitching his eyebrows as he looked up guiltily from one cross face to another. He gave a low, miserable whine, looking desperately ashamed of himself.

'How did he get at the basket?' Mr Hope asked, peering into the back of the Land-rover.

'The grille must have been loose,' Mrs Hope replied. 'He managed to push it aside and, well, the rest is history. And so is our picnic, I'm afraid.'

'Oh well, looks like we'll just have to have lunch in the café,' said Mr Hope, clearing up the remnants of the picnic. 'That's not such a huge tragedy, I suppose. Now, let's get this *bad dog* back in the Land-rover,' he said, winking at James.

James nodded. 'Up you get, Blackie,' he said seriously.

Blackie got slowly to his feet, tail still down, and pushed his head against James's leg, aware of the circle of stern faces staring down at him. He whimpered pathetically.

Mrs Hope's mouth began to twitch. 'I suppose you've got to see the funny side,' she said. 'Would you ever believe a dog could look so embarrassed? He'd like to dig a big hole and bury himself in it!'

Despite the pangs of hunger from her empty stomach, Mandy could feel the corners of her mouth twitching upwards too.

Mr Hope couldn't stand it any longer and let out a loud bellow of laughter.

Blackie immediately perked up, looking round hopefully at everyone.

'It's OK, Blackie,' James told him with a comforting pat. 'I think you've been forgiven.'

'Come on, then,' said Mrs Hope, opening up the back of the Land-rover for Blackie to jump back in. 'The café it is. I'll treat you all – out of my winnings!'

'Oh, did you win, Mum?' Mandy asked excitedly. 'Which horse did you pick?'

'Flame of Hope,' said her mother, smiling and flicking back her long red hair. 'I thought it was very appropriate.'

'Thanks, Mum, that was great,' said Mandy, pushing away her empty plate after a delicious lunch of cheese and vegetable pasty and chips.

Mrs Hope was studying the racecard. 'I think we should make a move if we're going to catch the two-thirty,' she said. 'So, are you going to choose Pilgrim's Progress for this race, Mandy?'

'I suppose so,' Mandy replied. 'Tom said he'd be a certainty if he was on form. We'll just have to hope he is.'

'Well, the yard hasn't had much luck so far today,' said her father. 'And still no sight of Mr Folan!' he added. 'It gives a terrible impression of the yard if he won't even turn up when his horses are running.'

'Poor Tom,' said Mandy. 'He's having a terrible time today. I wish there was something we could do to help.'

'Well, we can cheer Pilgrim's Progress on, for one thing,' said her mother. 'He's number six. The jockey's in pink-and-purple silks, I think, so it should be easy to spot him. Come on, let's get going.'

By the time they had threaded their way through the crowds and got to the paddock, the jockeys had already mounted.

'Oh, there he is!' James said, grabbing Mandy's elbow and pointing out the bay they'd seen at Folan's. 'Look, it says number six on the saddlecloth, and that must be Jim riding him.'

'There's Tom, too,' Mandy said. 'See, walking at his head. Oh, come on, Pilgrim!'

'He doesn't look very enthusiastic, does he?' James observed.

Mandy had to agree. Pilgrim's Progress was plodding along with his head down while Jim sorted out his reins and his whip. The jockey soon gathered him in, but he still looked like he'd rather have been anywhere else than on a racetrack.

'There they go!' said Mr Hope, as the horses began to file out of the paddock and canter over to take a look at the track. 'Come on, let's go to the Members' enclosure and watch from there. We might as well make the most of the passes Harry gave us.'

As the Hopes and James made their way to the enclosure, Mandy's eye was suddenly caught by a familiar figure inside. 'Hey, Dad!' she said, looking between two large ladies in fur coats. 'Isn't that Mr Johnson over there?'

Mr Hope followed her gaze. 'You're right, love,' he said. 'And I wonder who that is with him? Maybe it's our mystery man, Mr Folan. Come on, let's find out.' He began to ease his way through the crowd, Mandy and James following close behind him.

'I'll stay here,' Mrs Hope called after them. 'You don't need me hanging around.'

Harry Johnson was chatting to a younger, serious-looking man with sandy-coloured hair. Short and slight, if he'd been dressed differently he could have been mistaken for one of the jockeys.

'I think he's seen us,' Mandy said, as Mr Johnson looked in their direction, then waved.

'Good!' said Mr Hope. 'Let's go and introduce ourselves. I've got a few bones to pick with Mr Folan, if that's who he is.'

Mr Johnson spoke again to the younger man, who turned round and stared intently for a few seconds at Mr Hope, James and Mandy as they approached. Then he turned on his heel, ready to walk away.

Mr Johnson took the man's elbow, wanting him to stay. But the man shook off his arm, almost angrily, then quickly strode away through the crowd. In seconds he was swallowed up among the swarm of people.

Mandy stopped short. 'It looks like he's trying

to avoid us,' she said, bewildered.

'Surely it wouldn't hurt him just to meet us, would it?' James added.

'Well, he's made his feelings very clear,' Mr Hope said grimly. 'He's not even prepared to talk.'

Harry Johnson came over to them, looking embarrassed. 'I'm sorry,' he said. 'That was Mr Folan. I tried to get him to meet you, but he wasn't having any of it.'

'Doesn't he care what happens to his horses?' Mandy burst out.

'He does care – too much, if anything,' Mr Johnson replied. 'I just can't get him to face up to all the problems we're having. He seems to think if he ignores them they'll just go away.'

'But that's a recipe for disaster!' Mr Hope said. 'We've got to work together or the situation will never improve.'

'I know, I know,' said Mr Johnson, 'but I think we'll have to take it one step at a time. At least he came here today – a few weeks ago, I thought I'd never see him on a racetrack again!'

Just then, a bell rang. 'Oh!' said Mr Johnson. 'They're under starter's orders already.

We'll have to talk about this later.'

Mandy desperately tried to crane over the heads of the people around her. 'It's so crowded in here!' she said. 'I can't see a thing.'

'No offence, Mr Johnson,' James said, 'but would you mind if Mandy and I went down to the racetrack? I think we'd get a better view.'

'That's fine,' Mr Johnson replied, smiling. 'But you'd better hurry, or you'll miss the start.'

'Meet you back here!' Mr Hope called after them as they rushed out of the enclosure and down to the track.

James wriggled through a knot of people and found a gap by the railings near the starting line. 'Here, Mandy!' he shouted, saving a space for her.

In a second Mandy was beside him. 'There's Pilgrim!' she said, pointing to the line of horses. Pilgrim's Progress stood a little way apart, not fidgeting with excitement like the others, but still as a statue.

James and Mandy looked at each other, full of apprehension.

Suddenly the horse tensed, arching his neck and lifting his head up in the air. His nostrils flared and his eyes rolled. A startled, terrified look came over his face.

'Oh no!' Mandy cried. 'What's the matter with him?'

James shook his head anxiously.

Mandy could see that Jim had sensed a change in the horse too, but there was no time for him to react. The starters dropped the tape, and the race began. There was a huge roar from the crowd as the horses set off, and Pilgrim's Progress shot to the front immediately.

'He's breaking away too soon!' James shouted in her ear. 'He'll have nothing left for the finish at this rate!'

Mandy's hands were clenched into fists, pushed deep into her jacket pockets. She could see Jim was fighting to control the horse, and she silently urged him to slow down that headlong pace. Anything could happen if Pilgrim's Progress kept up such a wild gallop; both he and Jim might be badly hurt.

'Get yourself together, Pilgrim!' James cried, but the horse was away in a world of his own. He was out in front by a couple of lengths now, and approaching the first fence.

Mandy's nails dug into her palms, but she hardly noticed the pain. Her eyes were fixed on that one horse as she willed him up and over the jump. And then, suddenly, she gasped and grabbed James's elbow, transfixed as a flash of silvery white shone out, right behind Pilgrim's Progress.

'What was *that*?' James shouted in amazement.

And Mandy knew he'd seen it too. For a brief second, amongst the surging line of horses, the image of a massive grey stallion had appeared, tail streaming out behind him like a banner as

he flew over the ground. And then, just as
quickly, it was gone.

There was no time to think or talk about what
they had just seen. They both had to keep their
eyes on the racetrack and Pilgrim's headlong
rush. Approaching the fence, the horse seemed
to increase his speed. Then, at the very last
minute, as the brushwood towered up in front
of him, he veered sharply to the left.

There was a gasp from the crowd and
Mandy held her breath as they all saw Pilgrim's
Progress soar straight over the white railings
bordering the far side of the course. A couple
of track officials standing there scattered as he
bore down on them. Someone screamed, and
there were shouts of confusion and alarm from
the spectators.

'What's he doing?' James cried.

'He's escaping!' Mandy shouted back. 'Can
you see what's happening?' she asked James
frantically. Her view was blocked by a tall man
in a tweed jacket, scanning the view with a pair
of binoculars.

'I think Jim's pulled him up,' James said,
peering into the distance. 'And a few people

are running after them. Oh, there's Tom! They've got him back to a walk now.'

The crowd thinned as people started to walk up the track for a better view of the continuing race. James and Mandy were left staring at each other, wide-eyed.

'You saw him too, didn't you?' Mandy asked.

'Yes,' James replied, 'I did. It was Tibor – the horse that was put down, wasn't it?'

Mandy nodded.

Seven

The sky was gloomy and overcast as Mrs Hope drove home. Blackie was sleeping quietly in the back of the Land-rover. The enormous meal he'd eaten and a run round the carpark had tired him out.

Mandy listened to her parents chatting in the front seats. Both Mr Hope and the course vet had checked Pilgrim's Progress over thoroughly and he seemed to be unhurt, thank goodness, though he was very shaken.

She turned to James. 'Did you see the look on Pilgrim's face as the race began?' she asked him quietly. 'It was just the same as Hadrian's, when he came bolting into the yard that day.'

'So you think Hadrian had been spooked by Tibor too?' James said, pushing back his glasses seriously. 'It seems incredible, but maybe you're right. The horses must be able to feel him near them, and that's why they're all so frightened.'

'And he was here on the racetrack today, for certain,' Mandy said.

James nodded.

'You see, James – I *wasn't* imagining that horse in the field!' Mandy went on. 'It *must* have been Tibor.'

'But it doesn't look as if Tibor showed himself to anyone else at the racetrack today,' James pointed out, 'so who will believe us?' They had been amazed that no one else had spoken of seeing the flash of grey stallion at Pilgrim's heels during the two-thirty race.

Mandy sighed. 'Mr Johnson certainly won't want to hear about it,' she said, staring out of the window. 'Remember how cross he got with me last week?'

Then she turned and looked at James. 'But

I'll tell you who I think holds the key to all this,' she said. 'Mr Folan. He was riding Tibor just before he died. We've got to get in touch with him, James!'

'Yes, but how?' James asked. 'He won't come anywhere near us.'

'I'm not sure yet,' Mandy answered. 'We'll have to think up a plan.'

'Here we are – back home!' said Mrs Hope, as she turned the Land-rover into the Animal Ark driveway.

'And back to work, I bet,' added Mr Hope, hearing the phone ring as he came up to the front door. 'I wonder who this is?'

The call turned out to be from the owner of an Irish wolfhound, who'd just noticed a huge abscess on the side of his dog's face and wanted to bring her in straight away.

'And it might be a bit of a problem case,' explained Mr Hope. 'Apparently the dog is petrified of vets, so she's not going to come in here willingly. And she's a large lady! We may have to be a bit clever to get her inside.'

'I've got some of Blackie's dog treats in my

pocket. Do you think they might help?' James suggested.

'You never know!' smiled Mrs Hope. 'Why don't you have a go with those while we get the surgery ready?'

Fifteen minutes later, an estate car drew up outside the surgery. Mandy and James went out to meet the new patient, taking Blackie with them on the lead.

The wolfhound's owner, a short man with a worried expression, came round to open up the back of the car, which contained one of the biggest dogs Mandy and James had ever seen.

'This is Tiny,' the man said. Tiny was doing her best to cower into a corner, but, as she took up the whole space, it was impossible.

'Hello, Tiny,' said Mandy soothingly. 'We're not going to hurt you.'

'Hey, what about these, girl?' said James, holding out a couple of dog treats. The wolfhound gingerly stretched her head forward and smelled them, then turned her head away. Mandy and James gasped as they saw the poor dog's huge swollen cheek.

And then Tiny caught sight of Blackie,

peering nosily into the car, tail wagging.

The Labrador gave a short bark and started to cavort about, crouching down and then springing up again on the end of his lead. Tiny's eyes brightened with interest momentarily.

'Come on, Tiny,' said Mandy, 'come and play with Blackie!'

Tiny continued to stare at the friendly black Labrador. Then, very slowly and carefully, she uncoiled her long legs and began to struggle to her feet.

'Good girl!' Mandy said encouragingly, as she and Tiny's owner helped the huge dog down from the car.

Tiny and Blackie sniffed at each other. Blackie's tail was wagging furiously, and slowly, Tiny began to wave hers a little, too. Tiny's owner was looking very relieved as he closed the tailgate of his car.

'Good work, you two!' laughed Mr Hope from the doorway. 'James, if you could bring Blackie in, I think Tiny will follow. Just take him into the surgery and, with a bit of luck, Tiny won't even notice where she is.'

The plan worked perfectly, and Tiny was soon

safely installed in one of the treatment rooms with Mr and Mrs Hope and her owner. Blackie waited patiently outside the closed door.

'Don't worry, Blackie!' smiled Mandy. 'We'll take good care of your new friend, and I'm sure you can see her later.'

'Do you think he's made up for eating the picnic?' asked James.

Mandy nodded, grinning as they made their way back into the kitchen. Just then, the phone rang again. She picked up the receiver. 'Animal Ark. Can I help you?'

There was a crackling buzz on the other end of the line, then a voice said faintly, 'Hello? This is Gerald Folan here. To whom am I speaking?'

Mandy's heart thumped with excitement. *Gerald Folan – the owner of the stables!* Maybe this was their chance! She waved James to come over to the phone, silently mouthing, *'Mr Folan!'* James's eyes lit up and he hurried over to listen too.

Mandy cleared her throat. 'This is Mandy Hope, Mr Hope's daughter,' she answered politely. 'I'm afraid my father's in surgery at the moment, but I can get a message to him . . .'

She waited expectantly as the line crackled again.

'Please tell him that we're having more trouble with our horses,' came Mr Folan's business-like reply, 'and I be grateful if he could come out here as soon as possible.' There was a pause, then Mr Folan added, 'Would you be kind enough to accompany him, Mandy? He might need some assistance.'

'I'll pass the message on,' Mandy said eagerly. 'Shall I get my father to call you back?'

'No, thank you,' Mr Folan answered. 'It won't be possible for him to contact me. Just come as soon as you can, please.' And with that, the line went dead.

'Did you hear that, James?' Mandy asked excitedly as she scribbled down the message on to a pad by the phone. 'You should come along too, of course. We might get to meet Mr Folan at last!'

'I wonder what persuaded him to get involved with the stables again?' James asked curiously.

'Who knows,' Mandy replied. 'Maybe *he* saw Tibor this afternoon, too!'

* * *

'*Please* can we come to Folan's with you?' Mandy pleaded with her father. He'd just come out of the surgery and she'd eagerly passed on Mr Folan's message. 'Mr Folan said I should, and I'm sure James would be helpful too.'

'I don't know,' Mr Hope replied. 'Wouldn't you rather stay here and watch TV? It's been a long day for all of us.'

'We'd really rather see the horses again, Mr Hope,' said James seriously. 'And tomorrow's Sunday, so we can sleep in.'

'That's a point, I suppose,' Mr Hope admitted. He turned to Mandy. 'Oh, all right! I'll go and see what your mother says – she's still tidying poor old Tiny up.'

'Is Tiny going to be OK?' Mandy asked.

'I think so,' Mr Hope replied. 'We managed to cut the abscess out, but she needs a careful eye kept on her for the next couple of hours, to make sure she recovers from the anaesthetic OK. She'll be staying in the unit overnight.'

The verdict from the surgery was that Mandy and James could go with Mr Hope to Folan's, so long as they wrapped up warmly and stayed in the office if the horses were too unsettled.

Soon, they were in the Land-rover again, Mandy sitting beside her father and James in the back seat with a Thermos of hurriedly made hot chocolate and a pile of blankets.

Mr Hope turned the key in the ignition, but there was only a dull splutter in response. 'That's all we need!' he sighed, waiting a few seconds before trying again. Eventually, the engine started and they headed out of Welford towards Folan's.

'I hope there's nothing seriously wrong at the stables,' Mr Hope said, peering anxiously ahead into the gloom. 'They must have a pretty good reason for calling me out at night.'

'At least Mr Folan's talking to us now, though, Dad,' Mandy said. 'That's a good sign, isn't it?'

'We'll see when we get there,' Mr Hope replied. 'Frankly, I've got no idea what to expect.'

They drove on through a light shower of rain. Mandy listened to the swish, swish of the windscreen wipers and stared out into the darkness, letting her mind wander. She must have fallen asleep, because the next thing she knew she had woken up with a start from dreams of galloping grey stallions, bucking racehorses and timid Irish wolfhounds. The Land-rover had stopped.

'Are we there, Dad?' she yawned, rubbing her eyes while James stretched his arms in the back.

'No, we're not,' Mr Hope said grimly, trying to start the engine again. 'I'm afraid the Land-rover's decided to die on us.'

'What's happened?' James asked, craning forward from the back seat.

'I'm not sure,' Mr Hope said, 'I slowed down to take this corner and the Land-rover just conked out.' He turned the key in the ignition again and pressed hard on the accelerator, but the engine was completely dead. 'This is hopeless,' he said, giving up. 'It's not going to start.'

'So what do we do now?' Mandy asked.

'Well, I don't think we're too far away from Folan's,' her father replied. 'I'll just hop out and have a look around to try and see exactly where we are. We may be able to walk there, and we can ring a garage once we arrive.'

He opened the glove compartment and took out a sturdy rubber torch and a map. 'You guys stay here for the moment. Don't worry! I won't be long.' He opened the car door and jumped down.

Mandy saw his face in the torchlight as he gave them a thumbs-up sign. A second later, he had been swallowed up by the darkness. She and James stared at each other. The Land-rover lights weren't working, and they could only just see each other in the weak moonlight that came filtering through the window.

'Well, this is turning out to be even *more* exciting than we thought it would be!' James said.

Eight

'What's happened to Dad?' Mandy asked, peering out into the darkness around the Land-rover. 'Surely he should be back by now!'

'He's only been gone a little while,' James replied. He pressed a button on his digital watch and the flashing green numbers shone out brightly. 'Yes, just ten minutes.'

'Are you sure?' Mandy asked. 'Seems like much longer than that. I hate sitting here like this, not doing anything. Is there any more hot chocolate left?'

'No, it's all gone,' James said, shaking the

flask. 'Maybe we could just have a quick look outside to see where we are. At least it'll pass the time.'

Mandy opened the passenger door, letting in a cold gust of wind that ruffled her hair. She jumped down and, a few seconds later, James was standing beside her on the empty road.

It had stopped raining, but the odd flurry of raindrops was blown into their faces every now and then from the nearby trees. There was no sign of Mr Hope anywhere. Mandy narrowed her eyes, trying to see if she could spot any landmarks.

'Can you recognise anything?' she asked James, peering into the distance.

'I haven't a clue!' he replied. 'We could be anywhere.'

'Oh, there's Dad!' Mandy said thankfully, catching sight of a torchbeam dancing along the road towards them. 'Maybe he'll have some idea.'

'Well, from what I can make out, we're not a great distance from the stables,' Mr Hope told them. 'We could follow the road, but I think I've found a quicker route – through the woods.

I remember Harry Johnson telling me that the jockeys use it on their way to and from the gallops. The signpost is just up there on the right.' He looked questioningly at Mandy and James.

Mandy shivered, remembering what Mr Johnson had said about Hadrian getting spooked in the woods. Then she pulled herself together. 'If it's the quickest way to Folan's, then we should go through the woods,' she said firmly. James nodded.

'Right then,' said Mr Hope. He opened the rear door of the Land-rover, then reached in and took out his veterinary bag and a length of rope, which he wound around his shoulder. 'Best to be prepared!' he said cheerfully. 'Now let's get going.'

Mandy and James followed Mr Hope a short distance down the road, then he stopped and shone the torch on to a footpath leading into the wood. A wooden signpost pointing along it announced, 'Stables 1 mile'.

'Right, here we are,' he said. 'Stay close to me and careful how you go.'

They plunged into the wood, guided by the

flickering torchbeam. It was much darker here than on the road, as a thick canopy of leaves kept out the faint moonlight.

Mandy gazed into the dark undergrowth on either side of the path and shivered. Who knew what might be hidden behind the thick, rustling wall of leaves and branches?

Suddenly, a fierce wind picked up, tossing branches of trees above them this way and that. Stinging drops of rain began to splatter down into their faces as they walked doggedly on, following the path.

James turned round to Mandy. 'This is weird!' he said. 'There was no sign of a storm before we started on this path!'

Mandy nodded, but didn't speak. All her senses were alert. The air felt heavy and electric. Something was happening – but she didn't know what.

'Let's have a song!' Mr Hope called back, and struck up his own version of 'Ten Green Bottles'. But when Mandy and James showed no inclination to join in, he gave up.

They stumbled on in silence, Mr Hope occasionally calling, 'All right at the back?' to check they were both there.

'Maybe this isn't such a great adventure after all,' James grumbled, stopping to wipe his steamed-up glasses.

'Come on!' Mandy said sharply. 'The quicker we go, the quicker we'll get out of here!' She tried to keep the anxiety out of her voice, but didn't manage it.

'Are you all right?' James said, staring at her in surprise.

'I don't like this wood,' Mandy admitted. 'It just doesn't feel right.'

'Keep going, you two!' Mr Hope called from in front. He shone the torch back down the path to see where James and Mandy were. 'I think this storm is getting worse and I don't want you to fall behind.'

The storm certainly did seem to be getting worse. The wind had risen to a shriek, and Mandy's hair was whipping over her eyes. Branches creaked eerily overhead, and the low rumble of thunder moved threateningly over the sky above them.

Then Mandy became aware of another sound, hard to pick up above the storm at first. She grasped James's sleeve. 'Listen!' she said urgently. 'What's that?'

Her father had heard it too. Up ahead, something was crashing through the undergrowth. The three of them stood there, listening as the crashing, tearing sound drew louder and nearer. It seemed to be heading straight towards them. And then a frantic neighing sounded out. It was a horse.

'Let's get out of its path!' shouted Mr Hope, springing into action. He shepherded Mandy and James to the side of the path and stood with his arms round them. They stared anxiously into the darkness ahead. Then a huge, dark shape came hurtling round the corner. As it approached, Mr Hope called out, shone his torch in the creature's direction and stepped out on to the path.

Startled by the noise and the light, it skidded to a noisy halt.

'Hadrian!' cried James in amazement. 'What's *he* doing here?'

'Easy there, boy,' said Mr Hope soothingly as he approached the frightened horse. Hadrian shied backwards, snorting in alarm, but Mr

Hope carried on talking quietly, holding out one hand while he smoothly unhooked the rope from his shoulder.

Within a few seconds, he had tied it firmly to the horse's headcollar. 'This is getting to be a habit,' he said as he patted Hadrian's neck.

It took Mandy a few seconds to recover herself. The memory of the last terrifying time Hadrian had bolted towards her in Folan's yard had come flooding back.

'I thought Mr Johnson said Hadrian was frightened of the wood,' James observed. 'So why has he run away from the stables and come out here in the cold and rain? It doesn't make sense!'

'It does seem strange,' Mr Hope replied. 'Maybe there's been an accident up at the yard that we don't know about. Let's try and get there as quickly as we can. Just mind out while I turn Hadrian around.'

The horse was still trembling violently. As Mr Hope tried to wheel him around, he snorted in fear, dancing backwards and rolling his eyes so that the whites showed. 'Come on, Hadrian,' Mr Hope said. 'This way, there's a good lad.'

'He doesn't want to go back,' Mandy said, watching the terrified animal. 'It's like he's frightened of something up there, towards the stables.'

They all stared ahead, through the swaying trees. The wind was building up to gale force level, howling as it whipped the branches to and fro. Stinging drops of rain splattered down. There was a loud crack as a huge sheet of lightning lit up the sky, followed by a deafening crash of thunder, right overhead.

Mandy put her hands over her ears – then froze as she caught sight of a flash of white coming through the trees. She nudged James and pointed at it wordlessly.

James looked and his jaw dropped as another horse came fully into view. It seemed to glide over the ground, long mane rippling, its dazzling white coat almost luminous in the darkness.

'Oh!' Mandy breathed, as she watched the huge stallion come majestically down the path towards them and stop a few paces away. He stood there, watching them, one hind leg bent and resting on the tip of his hoof. The wind had died down a little, but flickers of lightning still shot through the clouds behind him and thunder rumbled overhead.

Hadrian was quiet now, almost paralysed with fear. Adam Hope stood next to him, also staring at the incredible sight of what could only be Tibor.

Somehow, the fear that had gripped Mandy slipped away. She was mesmerised, too fascinated to feel afraid of this amazing creature. And she could tell that he was in some kind of distress. It was as though waves of sadness were radiating out of him. Slowly, she stepped forward . . .

But Tibor suddenly turned, rearing up and kicking with his forelegs. Again and again, he lashed out against the stormy sky, as though his misery were turning to fury. It was something to behold: a stallion in the very eye of the storm.

Summoning up all her courage, Mandy carried on slowly towards him.

'Mandy! What are you doing?' cried her father, pulling her back.

'It's OK, Dad,' she said. 'Somehow, I know he's hurting – but he won't hurt me. He wants help.'

As if he'd heard her, the fight seemed to go out of Tibor. He dropped back on to all fours and gazed searchingly at Mandy with his dark, blazing eyes.

Slowly, she reached out and laid her hand on his neck. It was smooth as marble, icy cold to the touch.

'Quiet, boy!' she said softly, though her voice shook. 'Easy, there!'

Tibor blew down his nose and she felt the shock of his icy breath once again, just as she had done in the empty stall. She bravely grasped a handful of his mane. 'Come on, Tibor,' she said. 'We're going home.'

The horse looked at her silently, without moving. Then he bowed his head, as though giving up some heavy burden. With Mandy at his side, he turned and began to walk slowly back up the path.

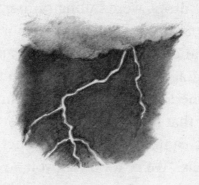

Nine

Mandy hardly dared to turn round and check that James and her father were following as she walked on beside Tibor. It had begun to rain again in earnest, but he moved smoothly, without once stumbling. He seemed to carry a centre of stillness with him, and Mandy felt certain he would lead them safely back to Folan's yard.

In the distance came threatening rumbles of thunder. The wind kept up its low moan, and she could hear the rain beating into the bushes that bordered the path. Somehow, though, hardly any drops were falling on her.

Mandy put her head closer to Tibor's massive shoulder and moved on, as if sleep-walking, wondering at the fact that she wasn't the least bit frightened. But Tibor meant them no harm. The anger that had poured out of him was gone.

'Mandy!' came a loud whisper at her shoulder. It was James. 'We're following you – your dad is leading Hadrian. Are we dreaming, or is this really happening?'

'I don't know!' Mandy whispered back. 'We can't all be having the same dream together, but I'm not sure what's going on! Just stay close behind us. How's Hadrian?'

'He seems to have calmed down a bit,' James replied. 'I'll tell your dad you're OK.' And he darted back down the path.

Mandy carried on walking, glancing up at Tibor from time to time as she went. She could understand what James meant. It *was* like a strange dream, walking through the darkness with the stallion beside her. Yet, at the same time, she felt that everything so far had been leading up to this point. Seeing Tibor in the field when they'd first come to Folan's, sensing him in the stall and then seeing him again on the racecourse – it was as though they'd been destined to meet. And maybe there was a reason for it.

Just then, the path widened out, and soon Mandy found herself at the main gate into Folan's stables. She risked a quick look back, and saw James and her father standing a little way behind, Hadrian next to them. They watched her silently, waiting to follow her lead.

Tibor hesitated for a moment, but she urged him forward with one hand on his neck. 'Come on,' she said. 'Don't give up now!'

Together they walked through the gates, while the wind howled around them. The place was in uproar! Lights were blazing out of the office windows, and a confused babble of sound rose on the air as people shouted, stable doors banged and frantic horses neighed. Queenie was running to and fro, barking wildly.

The storm had obviously caused some damage: guttering had been torn off the office wall and hung at a crazy angle, and smashed roof tiles lay all over the ground. Whole sections of fencing had been blown down around the paddock, too.

Mandy and Tibor carried on into the yard and stood there for a moment. James, Adam Hope and Hadrian followed and they stood together, a quiet centre in the midst of the storm. Mandy looked at her father.

'Are you all right, love?' his questioning glance said. She smiled back her answer.

Tibor's long silky mane floated over his neck, seeming to flow and shimmer with each gust of wind. He stared towards the barn, his ears pricked forward, and then shook his head, almost impatiently.

At once the storm calmed, dropping to a low murmur. The crashing and banging of stable doors died away and the neighs and squeals of the horses faded into a tense, unnatural silence.

Mandy saw Harry Johnson rush out of the barn, closely followed by Tom and a young man who must have been another of the stable lads. When they caught sight of Tibor, they stopped dead in their tracks.

Stumbling a little, the stable manager walked slowly down to the yard towards them, his face pale and his eyes wide with shock as he stared at Tibor.

'I don't believe it . . .' Mandy heard him say, his voice sounding as though it came from very far away. He looked at each of their faces, trying to work out what could possibly be happening.

Then Tibor began to head up the slope towards the barn where the other horses were kept. Mandy walked beside him, but she could sense that he was hardly aware of her any more. He was staring straight ahead. She felt him falter for a second, but then he glided on, hardly seeming to touch the ground as he went.

Tom and the other lad stood back to one side as they passed, looking terrified. As they reached the entrance to the barn, dimly lit by a yellowish overhead light, Mandy drew in her breath at what she saw. All the horses were completely still and silent, staring at Tibor expectantly.

Tibor looked round at them, then moved calmly forward. Mandy stayed where she was, watching. She knew where the stallion was heading and, sure enough, he made straight for the stall with deep hoofprints gouged out of its door. His own stall.

'Are you OK, Mandy?' said a quiet voice at her shoulder. It was James.

'Yes, I'm fine,' she whispered back. 'I just don't know what's going to happen now.'

'I don't think anybody does,' James replied. 'Mr Johnson nearly passed out when he saw you with Tibor.'

Mandy looked around. Behind her and James, a ring of anxious, disbelieving faces had gathered, staring into the barn. Mr Hope had led Hadrian up with him and the horse stood quietly at his shoulder, quite calm now.

And then, as Tibor came to a halt outside his stall, Mandy gasped as the door slowly opened and a figure emerged. Mandy recognised the man from seeing him briefly at the races. It was Mr Folan.

He gazed at Tibor, transfixed, and then, almost timidly, he stretched up an arm towards the stallion's head.

Slowly, solemnly, the huge stallion arched his proud neck and bowed down to meet Mr Folan's hand. A radiant smile lit up the man's face.

For long seconds, the two stood silently together. And then, at last, as Mr Folan finally let his hand fall to his side again, Tibor wheeled round and cantered back out of the barn.

All the onlookers scattered as the stallion came towards them, but he seemed to float through them. Passing Mandy and James, he bowed his head, then went on – out into the dark night.

Suddenly, everything was noise and confusion again. Mr Hope quickly gave Hadrian to Tom and rushed up to Mandy. Queenie had appeared from somewhere and was barking furiously at her ankles, and James was talking excitedly.

'Stand back! Give her some air!' she heard her father say as she staggered against the wall.

Mandy shook her head, trying to clear the mist that was making it swim. 'It's OK – I'm fine,' she muttered, as anxious faces stared down into hers. She looked over to Tibor's stall where the solitary figure of Mr Folan was still standing, watching. 'Really, I'm fine,' she said again. 'But I need to talk to Mr Folan!' She looked pleadingly up at her father, who nodded.

'I'd better go and check on the horses, love, if you're sure you're all right,' he said. Then he turned to James. 'Go with Mandy, will you? I'll be as quick as I can.'

James nodded, and Mr Hope hurried back over to the barn.

Everyone else melted away as Mandy and James walked slowly towards Mr Folan.

He came forward to meet them, standing at the entrance of the barn. 'You brought Tibor here,' he said, eyes shining with emotion. 'How did it happen? How did you do it?'

Mandy looked at James. 'I don't really know how,' she said, haltingly. She tried to explain. 'I've caught glimpses of him a couple of times before this evening,' she began. 'Then tonight, we had to come through the woods because the Land-rover broke down. And while we were there, Tibor arrived and decided to let us see him . . . But I think he's always been here – waiting for the right time . . .'

'And we think the horses knew he was around,' James added. 'That's why they've been so jumpy.'

Mr Folan nodded. Then he sighed sadly.

'I couldn't face coming back here after the accident,' he confided quietly. 'Not with everyone staring at me and knowing what I'd done. I couldn't face the other horses, either. I knew how upset and frightened they had become – but I just didn't know what to do about it.'

'So Tibor's ghost hadn't shown himself to you before tonight?' Mandy asked. 'You didn't glimpse him on the racetrack today, during the two-thirty?'

Mr Folan shook his head. 'I left before the race started,' he said. 'Just after I saw you there, with your father. Harry told me who you were, but I'm afraid I couldn't face meeting you,' he confessed, looking embarrassed. 'Well, well,' he continued. 'So Tibor was there too?'

James nodded. 'We saw him behind Pilgrim's Progress – just for a second.'

'It's as if Tibor couldn't bear to let a Folan's horse run a race without him,' Mandy mused out loud. 'But unfortunately, it just spooked the other horses.'

Mr Folan gazed into the barn. 'So that's what's been happening . . .' he said, deep in thought.

Then he turned to Mandy and James and smiled. 'But I think it's finished now. I looked into his eyes, and there was no anger there. He's forgiven me, I'm sure of that. And now he's gone – at peace at last.'

'I think you're right,' Mandy said, smiling back. 'This place feels different already, doesn't it?'

They looked down the wide central aisle. The wind whistled in through gaping holes in the roof that the storm had caused, swirling the odd wisp of hay. But that bone-numbing eerie chill they'd felt earlier was gone. A couple of horses whinnied across the corridor to each other, and nearly every loose box had a friendly, inquisitive face gazing out of it.

'Look, Hadrian's happier too,' James said. Hadrian nodded his lovely chestnut head, his long mane rippling, as though he agreed. They all laughed, watching him pull a mouthful of hay out of the net.

Mandy thought back to the moment she'd first seen Hadrian, galloping into the yard in a panic. He was a different animal now.

Suddenly, Mr Folan looked sad again. 'It's

funny how things work out ... I came here tonight to tell Harry I've decided to sell up,' he told them. 'But we never got around to having the conversation, with all that was happening!' He began to walk towards the office, saying, 'I suppose I should tell him now ...'

Mandy and James followed him, appalled.

'But you can't do that!' James exclaimed. 'Not now everything's come right!'

'This is your chance to start again,' Mandy added, laying her hand on Mr Folan's arm. She was horrified to think that he might give up now. It was as though everything they'd done had been for nothing!

Mr Folan halted and turned to look back into the barn. They watched as Mr Hope tended to the strawberry roan, Double-Decker. Hadrian was looking across to see what was going on. Jupiter, the young chestnut whom they'd met first at the yard, was giving the horse in the next stall a playful nibble, and Pilgrim's Progress was quietly dozing off, his lower lip drooping.

Mandy felt as though she'd come to know them all, even in such a short space of time.

'This is the horses' home!' she appealed to him. 'Where would they go?'

'Oh, their owners would soon find another trainer happy to take them,' Mr Folan replied. 'Some of them are threatening to do that already and, to be honest, I can't really blame them, under the circumstances. It's been awful to see the horses doing so badly. They'd probably be better off somewhere else.'

He sighed, and then turned to Mandy and James. 'But look, I haven't even thanked you or

Mr Hope for what you've done,' he said apologetically. 'It was so fortunate that you decided to call by when you did.'

Mandy looked at James, puzzled. 'Hang on a minute,' she said. 'We came because you asked us to.'

Now it was Mr Folan's turn to look surprised. '*I* asked you to? What do you mean?'

'I answered the phone,' Mandy told him. 'You said you were having more trouble with the horses and that you wanted us to come out here as soon as possible. Gerald Folan – that's you, isn't it?'

All the colour drained out of Mr Folan's face. '*Gerald* Folan, did you say? *Gerald*?' he repeated. 'Are you absolutely sure about that?'

'Yes I am – positive,' Mandy replied, growing more and more puzzled. 'Why? What's the matter?'

'Gerald Folan is my father,' Mr Folan said, faintly. 'Or rather, he was. He died a few months ago. My name is *Edward* Folan.'

'But that's impossible!' James said.

Mr Folan slowly shook his head and leaned against the barn doorway for support. 'So many amazing things are happening I can't begin to take them in. First Tibor, and now this . . .'

'It was a crackly line, but I remember his exact words,' Mandy declared. 'He said that he was Gerald Folan, and that my father should come out here this evening, as soon as possible – and that I should come too, to help.'

'Hey – maybe that's it!' said James.

Mandy and Mr Folan turned to look at him questioningly.

'Don't you see?' James went on. He looked at Mandy, then turned to Edward Folan. 'Somehow your father knew that Mandy was the key. She *was* the first one to see Tibor, after all. Perhaps Tibor had been waiting for someone he could trust – and he had chosen Mandy. And Mandy had to be here for Tibor to feel safe enough to show himself – to make his peace with you . . .' James finished breathlessly.

For a few seconds Edward Folan was speechless, his eyes filled with emotion. His voice was hoarse and cracked when, eventually, he said, 'You know, I think you could be right. It all makes sense, in an amazing, incredible sort of way . . .' He paused and looked at Mandy and James.

Mandy smiled at him, encouraging him to go on.

'My father loved these stables,' Mr Folan continued. 'They meant everything to him. He would never have let them leave the family when he was alive.'

'And he won't let you give them up now!' Mandy exclaimed. 'Oh, well done, James! You've worked it all out perfectly.' She turned to Mr Folan. 'You can't possibly sell up now, can you?'

There was a long silence as Mr Folan considered. 'No, I don't suppose I can,' he said eventually. 'Not with my father – and you two – against the idea!' he smiled. 'I'll just have to do my best to turn Folan's back into the stables it used to be. It's going to be hard work, though.'

'But everyone will want to help you,' Mandy said. 'There's Mr Johnson and Tom, and my father too, while he's here. They all want the yard to succeed. You can do it, I know you can! For Tibor's sake, as well as your own . . .' she finished quietly.

Edward Folan nodded. 'I'd say it was about

time I met your father,' he said. 'We'll have plenty to talk about over the next few days. There's work to be done!' And, throwing an arm round their shoulders, he walked with Mandy and James over to Mr Hope.

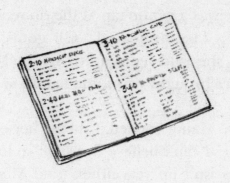

Ten

Slowly, Mandy opened her eyes, unsure for a moment where she was. Then she focused on the alarm clock beside her bed. It was nearly midday. She sat bolt upright in a sudden panic, before falling back on the pillows. Of course! Today was Sunday – she could sleep as long as she wanted. She closed her eyes again and thought back over everything that had happened the night before. Lying there in her familiar bedroom, it was hard to believe that she had even seen Tibor, let alone walked along beside him through the stormy night.

There was a gentle tap at the door, and her mother's face appeared. 'Oh good, you're awake,' she said, coming to sit on Mandy's bed. 'I've brought you some tea. How do you feel?'

'Dozy,' Mandy replied, rubbing her eyes and yawning. 'I can't believe I've slept so long!'

'James isn't up yet, either,' said Mrs Hope, putting the steaming mug on Mandy's bedside table. 'Well, you were very late home last night. I was getting so worried! But you certainly came back in style.'

'We did, didn't we,' Mandy smiled. 'It's not every day you get to ride in a breakdown truck! Have you talked to Dad about what happened yesterday?'

'Yes, I have,' said her mother. 'He told me about the storm, and the horse you met in the woods, and how you brought it back to the stables. But surely it couldn't have been the stallion that was put down, Mandy? That's just impossible! You don't really believe that, do you?'

'Yes, Mum, I do,' Mandy replied. 'I'm sure of it! But anyway – all that really matters is that the troubles at Folan's seem to have sorted out.'

'Well, your father doesn't know what to think,' said Mrs Hope, stroking Mandy's hair. 'He doesn't know if he's coming or going. Mr Folan rang first thing this morning, and kept him on the phone for nearly an hour.'

'Oh? What about?' Mandy said, sitting up.

'About his plans for the yard, apparently,' her mother said. 'The staff he's going to get to help with training and exercising, and how many more stable lads they need. Your father thinks he and Harry Johnson must have sat up talking half the night.'

'They've got a lot of catching up to do,' Mandy said, sipping her tea thoughtfully. 'Is Dad going over there again today?'

'No, that's the other thing Mr Folan was talking about,' Mrs Hope replied. 'There's a very good equine vet Harry Johnson's heard of, and he wanted to find out whether we knew anything about her.'

'And do you?' Mandy asked.

'Funnily enough, she trained with me at college,' said Mrs Hope. 'I've had news about her from time to time, but I never realised she'd come to practise up here. She's got an excellent reputation.'

'But Dad's only just started looking after the horses!' Mandy exclaimed.

'Well, it was always going to be a temporary arrangement,' replied her mother. 'I think Dad only agreed because Mr Johnson was just desperate for some help. It'll be much better for the yard to have a specialist equine vet, and Dad hasn't really got time to give them the attention they need. Especially not if they're going to expand.'

'But I was looking forward to going up there again,' said Mandy, disappointed. She really wanted to see Mr Folan and find out how the horses were doing.

'Well, don't despair,' smiled her mother. 'They're racing again this Saturday, and Mr Folan's promised us tickets. He says it's the least he can do.'

'Oh, can we go, Mum?' Mandy said eagerly. 'And can James come with us?'

'Well, I don't see why not,' her mother replied. 'But I think he'd better leave Blackie at home this time, don't you?'

* * *

The next Saturday, they were back in the racecourse carpark.

'This is perfect!' Mandy sighed, leaning against the wheel of the Land-rover and turning up her face to catch the last faint rays of the sun. 'This is how it should have been last week.'

'It certainly is,' smiled Mrs Hope. 'I love Blackie dearly, but it's a lot easier to eat a picnic without him. Have another sandwich, James.'

'Thanks, but I couldn't eat another thing,' James replied. 'I've had about six already!'

'I think we should make a move,' Mr Hope said. 'I promised we'd meet Mr Folan in the Members' enclosure at two. Come on, we'd better go and pick those tickets up.'

'How are things going at the yard?' Mandy asked her father as they walked over to the entrance gate. 'Have you heard from Mr Folan?'

'Only every day this week,' he replied, shaking his head. 'First he won't come near me, and now he won't leave me alone! I'll be quite glad when his new vet takes over, I must say.'

'Has Sharon agreed to start, then?' Mrs Hope asked.

'Apparently,' Mr Hope replied. 'I should think she'll be just what they need up there. But I shouldn't complain. It's great they've decided to make a go of the yard.'

'Did Mr Folan tell you which horses are racing today?' James asked.

'He said they're giving Pilgrim's Progress another chance,' Mr Hope said. 'You remember, Emily – the horse who jumped out of the course last week.'

'I'm surprised they've decided to race him again so soon,' Mrs Hope said. 'Do you think he'll be OK?'

'Well, I don't think Edward would have put him in for the race if he didn't have a chance,' Mr Hope replied. 'We'll just have to cross our fingers.'

'It's amazing,' Mandy said to James as they walked towards the Members' enclosure. 'Only a week has gone by since we were last here. It feels like a lifetime ago.'

'I know,' he replied. 'I wonder how Pilgrim will get on? Do you really think he'll be ready for this?'

'We'll soon find out,' Mandy said. 'Oh, there's Mr Folan!'

He was standing talking to a tall woman with dark curly hair. 'Emily!' she said as the Hopes approached, and rushed forward to give Mrs Hope a hug.

'I can see there's no need to introduce you two,' said Mr Folan, smiling. 'Mandy, James – meet Sharon Taylor, Folan's new vet. And Sharon, this is Adam Hope, who's been keeping your seat warm,' he joked.

'It's great to meet you,' she said, shaking Mr Hope's hand warmly. 'Thanks for keeping things ticking over.'

'And how are you both?' said Mr Folan, drawing James and Mandy a little to one side. 'Have you recovered from last weekend?'

'Oh, we're fine,' Mandy replied. 'It's great to see you looking so happy. I wondered whether you might have changed your mind about the yard.'

'Certainly not!' he replied. 'It feels like I've been in exile – and now I've come home. There's so much I want to do, and Sharon has lots of ideas. We're going to make Folan's the best yard in the country!'

'And how are the horses?' James asked. 'Do you think Pilgrim's Progress has got a good chance?'

'I've been amazed at the change in all of them,' Mr Folan replied. 'You wouldn't believe it. Sharon says Pilgrim's fit, and I wanted to put him back on the track again as soon as possible. We'll just have to see how he gets on. He's just gone off to the paddock if you want a look.'

'Oh, let's go over there, James!' Mandy said. She couldn't wait to see Pilgrim. 'We'll come back here for the race, Mr Folan.'

'You do that,' he said. 'I'll be over at the paddock myself in a minute. And call me Edward, please.' He flashed them both a smile. 'And thanks again, for everything you've done. Words don't seem enough, somehow. I'm just so glad you brought Tibor back.'

'Oh, it wasn't us,' Mandy said, embarrassed. 'He was the one who made everything happen. We'll see you later!' And she and James darted off through the crowd towards the paddock.

'There he is!' James said, and they watched as Pilgrim's Progress walked proudly around the ring, picking up his fine long legs and tossing his head with its sweeping black mane.

'Oh, isn't he lovely!' Mandy breathed. 'But I wonder how he's going to run – that's the main thing.'

'He looks like he really wants to race today,' said James. 'Do you remember how miserable he was in the ring last time?'

'You don't want to be bothering with that one,' snorted a woman in a tweed jacket and headscarf, standing next to them at the rails. 'He doesn't stand a chance – completely unreliable! No, Heaven Sent's a certainty for this race. She's the favourite, on at 3–1. Look, there she is.'

The woman pointed to a spirited-looking mare, whose jockey was having trouble reining her back. She was snorting, and clearly couldn't wait to get going, stamping the ground with her strong legs.

Mandy felt her heart sink. And then she saw Mr Folan, talking earnestly to Jim as the jockey prepared to swing up on to the horse's back. They both looked absolutely determined. 'Do your best, Pilgrim,' she whispered. 'For everyone's sake!'

'Watching them is making me even more nervous!' James said. 'Let's go and bag a good place down at the track. It's much more fun than the enclosure, and we can go straight back there after the race.'

They hurried over to the white railings and waited for the jockeys to ride their mounts over to the starting tape. All around them was a buzz of conversation as people looked at their racecards and discussed the odds.

'Here they come!' Mandy cried, as all eyes focused on the group of horses cantering slowly over to the starting line. Sunshine danced off their glossy coats and gleamed on jangling bits and stirrup irons.

'It's so exciting, but it's so nerve-wracking, too!' she said to James. 'I wonder how the jockeys are feeling?'

She searched for Pilgrim's Progress amongst the fidgeting, shifting row of horses and eventually spotted him – just as the tape dropped and the race began. With a roar from the crowd, the horses surged out on to the empty track in a thundering group and galloped towards the first fence.

A commentary was booming out over the track through several speakers dotted along it. From what they could make out, Pilgrim's Progress was lying fourth or fifth. It was almost impossible to keep track of one individual horse in that confusion of brown, chestnut, black and bay bodies, churning up the racetrack.

'Come on, Pilgrim!' Mandy shouted anyway. 'You can do it!' They watched as the horses disappeared around the corner, a blur of speed and pounding hooves. Spectators began to drift down the course, looking for other good vantage points.

'This way!' James said, tugging her to one side. 'Let's go to the finishing line and wait for them there.'

Several other people had the same idea, and Mandy and James had to thread their way through a jostling crowd, all staring down the track. At last they heard a distant thundering as the horses approached.

'And it's Heaven Sent from Madagascar, with Pilgrim's Progress coming up on the outside,' rang out the commentator's plummy voice.

'Yes!' shouted James and Mandy together.

'Go, Pilgrim! You can make it!'

'Come on, Heaven Sent!' bellowed a voice next to them, and they looked round to see the tweedy headscarved woman, her face flushed in anticipation of her winnings.

The hurtling group of horses and jockeys had now swept around the bend towards them, and everyone was surging forward to identify the leaders.

'And Madagascar's falling behind,' boomed the commentary. 'It's Heaven Sent, followed by Pilgrim's Progress, well out in front as they all come down to the final fence.'

The dark brown mare was leading by a couple of lengths, and looked like she would cruise to victory. Behind her came Pilgrim's Progress, every muscle and tendon in his body stretched to its fullest and his head straining forward as Jim stood up in the stirrups, crouching low over the horse's neck.

'Pilgrim! Come on!' Mandy screamed. She could hardly bear to watch, yet she couldn't look away as the gap between the two horses narrowed with each agonising second.

'Yes! You can do it! Go, Pilgrim!' James

shouted next to her. The valiant horse was closing in, finding an extra spurt of strength from some hidden reserve.

'Come on, Heaven Sent! Go for it, girl!' bellowed Mrs Headscarf, beside herself with excitement.

But now Heaven Sent seemed to be tiring. Her jockey urged her on, though it was clear she didn't have much more to give. The crowd erupted into a frenzy of cheering as the two horses approached the finishing line, neck and neck. Mandy couldn't hear herself think as she kept her eyes fixed on them both, willing Pilgrim's Progress to win with every fibre of her being, cheering with all her might.

And then it was all over. The horses were past the post and Pilgrim's Progress was slowing to an exhausted canter as Jim patted his neck proudly. 'Has he done it?' Mandy asked James frantically. 'Has he won?'

'And what an amazing finish!' crowed the commentator. 'It's Pilgrim's Progress by a nose from Heaven Sent, followed by Madagascar in third place.'

'Yes!' Mandy cried joyfully as she heard the

news, giving James a high five. 'Pilgrim's Progress, in first place! Oh, James, let's go and see him!'

They rushed over towards the knot of people clustering around Pilgrim's Progress as he made his way towards the winners' enclosure. Mr Folan was already walking along beside the horse, with the broadest grin Mandy had ever seen plastered over his face.

'Mandy, James!' he said, waving them over as soon as he saw them. 'We did it!'

'Pilgrim did it, you mean,' Mandy said, laughing, as she patted the horse's steaming neck. 'And Jim, of course,' she added, looking up at the triumphant jockey as he reached down to shake hands with yet another well-wisher.

'But they wouldn't have had the chance if it wasn't for you two,' Mr Folan said. 'This is a new beginning for Folan's stables, I know it. I'll never be able to thank you enough, never.'

'I think we had someone else on our side today, don't you?' Mandy said.

'Definitely,' Mr Folan answered, looking serious for a moment. 'I've been feeling him with me, every step of the way. I'll never forget

him, but the memories are happy ones now.'

Suddenly, Mandy's eye was caught by a tiny flash of silver-white. She turned to look, already knowing what she'd see. There in the distance, high up on the hill behind the racetrack, was a gleaming white stallion. 'Look!' she breathed. 'There! Up on the hill.'

Mr Folan and James followed her pointing finger. As they watched, the stallion reared up, then kicked up its heels and galloped over the brow of the hill, its tail streaming out behind like a banner.

'There he goes!' James cried.

'Goodbye, Tibor,' Mandy said softly. 'Now you can rest in peace.'

PONY IN THE POST
Animal Ark Christmas Special

Lucy Daniels

Mandy Hopes loves animals more than anything else. She knows quite a lot about them too: both her parents are vets and Mandy helps out in their surgery, Animal Ark.

A wrong delivery at Animal Ark brings a big surprise – the tiniest horse that Mandy has ever seen! The Miniature Horse was meant for Tania Benster, a newcomer to Welford. But Tania's parents have just divorced and she's too upset to care about her gift. Can Mandy show Tania how much this little horse has to offer?

ANIMAL ARK *by Lucy Daniels*

All Hodder Children's books are available at your local bookshop, or can be ordered direct from the publisher. Just tick the titles you would like and complete the details below. Prices and availability are subject to change without prior notice.

Please enclose a cheque or postal order made payable to *Bookpoint Ltd*, and send to: Hodder Children's Books, 39 Milton Park, Abingdon, OXON OX14 4TD, UK. Email Address: orders@bookpoint.co.uk

If you would prefer to pay by credit card, our call centre team would be delighted to take your order by telephone. Our direct line *01235 400414* (lines open 9.00 am–6.00 pm Monday to Saturday, 24 hour message answering service). Alternatively you can send a fax on *01235 400454*.

TITLE		FIRST NAME		SURNAME	

ADDRESS	
DAYTIME TEL:	POST CODE

If you would prefer to pay by credit card, please complete: Please debit my Visa/Access/Diner's Card/American Express (delete as applicable) card no:

Signature ....

Expiry Date: ....

If you would NOT like to receive further information on our products please tick the box. ❐